*H*azel and Chloë Pound, on their eleventh birthday, found Marie Stopes and Havelock Ellis in their wardrobe. To be more precise, in the brush and comb shelf which was, together with a little mirror, on the inside of the left-hand door. The two girls immediately hid them both, pushing them well down behind the shoes, and the jigsaw puzzles which neither of them wanted to make. They did not realise, at the time, that their mother must have *planted* Stopes and Ellis in order for them to be found.

Hazel and Chloë, with polite mirth, were explaining this laughable incident to the Professor and his mother, the Lady Delaware Carpenter, during a pre-wedding tea party when their mother, whose tea party it was, came untidy and rather late to the tea table, drawing off her gardening gloves and explaining how the girls read both books in what they thought was complete secrecy. Sitting down, she placed her gardening shoes beside her chair and reminded her daughters of the amusing fact that they were unable, at that time, to pronounce the word 'mutual'. And, because this word occurred so often in both books, the girls naturally thought this word was the correct word for sex. '*Mutual pleasure mutual happiness*', the word 'mutual' rolled roundly off her tongue as a part of a pealing laugh.

The Professor (who, of course, was not professorial then) often remembers that his mother had said how convenient it was that the girls were thus educated because, regrettably, she had completely overlooked this side of things in the upbringing of her own children though she supposed that both of them Delaware (the Prof.) and Delia, his sister, each in their own way being steeped in the Ancient Classics and in the study of Elizabethan (Renaissance) poetry and literature, could be looked upon as having encountered Stopes and Ellis but in different centuries.

She then, with a gracious smile, remarked on the

PENGUIN BOOKS

# AN ACCOMMODATING SPOUSE

Elizabeth Jolley was born in the industrial Midlands of England and moved to Western Australia in 1959. She is acclaimed as one of Australia's leading writers and has received an Order of Australia, honorary doctorates from WAIT (now Curtin University) and Macquarie and Queensland universities, and the ASAL Gold Medal for her contribution to Australian literature, as well as many major Australian awards for her fiction.

Her work includes short fiction, a collection of essays and fourteen novels, of which *The Well* won the Miles Franklin Award, *Mr Scobie's Riddle* and *My Father's Moon* the *Age* Book of the Year Award and *The George's Wife* the National Book Council Award for Fiction.

ALSO BY ELIZABETH JOLLEY

Stories
*Five Acre Virgin*
*The Travelling Entertainer*
*Woman in a Lampshade*
*Fellow Passengers*

Novels
*Palomino*
*The Newspaper of Claremont Street*
*Mr Scobie's Riddle*
*Miss Peabody's Inheritance*
*Foxybaby*
*Milk and Honey*
*The Well*
*The Sugar Mother*
*My Father's Moon*
*Cabin Fever*
*The Georges' Wife*
*The Orchard Thieves*
*Lovesong*

Non-fiction
*Central Mischief*
*Off the Air*
*Diary of a Weekend Farmer*

# ELIZABETH JOLLEY

## AN ACCOMMODATING SPOUSE

PENGUIN BOOKS

Penguin Notes for Reading Groups are available for this title.

Penguin Books Australia Ltd
487 Maroondah Highway, PO Box 257
Ringwood, Victoria 3134, Australia
Penguin Books Ltd
Harmondsworth, Middlesex, England
Penguin Putnam Inc.
375 Hudson Street, New York, New York 10014, USA
Penguin Books Canada Limited
10 Alcorn Avenue, Toronto, Ontario, Canada M4V 3B2
Penguin Books (NZ) Ltd
Cnr Rosedale and Airborne Roads, Albany, Auckland, New Zealand
Penguin Books (South Africa) (Pty) Ltd
5 Watkins Street, Denver Ext. 4, 2094, South Africa
Penguin Books India (P) Ltd
11, Community Centre, Panchsheel Park, New Delhi 110 017, India

First published by Penguin Books Australia Ltd 1999
This edition published by Penguin Books Australia Ltd 2000

1 3 5 9 10 8 6 4 2

Design by Ellie Exarchos, Penguin Design Studio
Cover illustration by Priscilla Nielsen
Typeset in 12.5/18 Perpetua by Midland Typesetters, Maryborough, Victoria
Printed in Australia by Australian Print Group, Maryborough, Victoria

National Library of Australia
Cataloguing-in-Publication data:

Jolley, Elizabeth, 1923 –.
An accommodating spouse.

ISBN 0 14 028817 1.

I. Title.

A823.3

www.penguin.com.au

I would like to express my thanks to Curtin University of Technology for the continuing privilege of being with students and colleagues in the School of Communication and Cultural Studies and for the provision of a room in which to write.

A special thanks is offered to Kay Ronai for editorial advice and corrections. Special thanks as well to Nancy McKenzie who continues to type my manuscripts.

And to all at Penguin Books Australia: thank you.

*Blame no one. Blame, if you must, the human situation.*

W. H. Auden

*The unexamined life is not worth living.*

Socrates

excellent quality of Mrs Pound's gardening gloves, asking if and where they could be purchased locally . . .

'These two women,' the Lady Delaware Carpenter said in her well-bred (county) resounding whisper, as they left Mrs Pound's comfortable, shabby house, 'these two women are so alike. It's impossible to tell which one is which. I do hope, Delaware, that you can tell them apart. I do hope,' she bellowed, 'that you will marry the right one. You do . . . distinguish between them . . .?' Her questioning voice was ringing like a village church bell when doubling as a fire alarm.

'Ultimately, Delaware, you will actually have to be able to recognise which one is your wife.'

*C*ertainly it is when he (Professor Delaware Carpenter), the father, considers shoulders he immediately recalls a night years ago when, inviting Hazel to accompany him to the opera *The Marriage of Figaro*, he discovered that the invitation had been understood to include Chloë, Hazel's twin sister, *and* their mother. The Professor (this was before he was Professor), with surprising presence of mind, stood well-dressed and handsomely smiling while the usher – looking like an opera goer himself in evening dress (dinner jacket and black tie) – suggested, if they would accept it, they could take standing room, easily procured for them at the back of the dress circle, until the first interval when those who were simply putting in an appearance acknowledging the presence of others would be leaving the performance. He, with a little smile, noticing the notes crushed in the Professor's hand, told them that, straight away, he could think of an expected four consecutive seats being vacant immediately with the first curtain.

It was during the occupation of the standing room that the Professor, immediately partly behind his lady guests, was able to study the substantial shoulders of his future wife, his future sister-in-law and, naturally, his future mother-in-law.

The three women in layered brocade – the raised pattern of the cloth enriched in the subdued lighting – displayed in the then fashionable backless dresses well-built magnificent shoulders, the outcome he thought of good breeding and early bedtime, horses and lots of open-air exercise at probably one of the better English boarding schools.

Without knowing then, as he came to know later, there was a tremendous dedication and skill required for the drafting of the block bodice, in the first place, on paper, and then there was the designing and the cutting out of the required style of the dress. Every new dress made especially for the particular occasion.

And every design springing from the homemade pattern.

He admired, on this evening, as he breathed in the heavy drenchings of perfume, the courage needed to wear such ugly dresses which exposed so much splendid and intimate flesh . . . All this clearly having no special effect on those others who were standing close by during the waiting for the comfortable seats recently promised . . .

When the Professor discovered that his sister-in-law was called Chloë and not Clover, he, for once issuing a command, declared that she was always to be, in the future, known as Chloë, it being a special name with a delicate meaning. Clover, he said at the time, was suitable only for a pet cow or a rabbit. Rabbits, in particular, could be called Clover. Hazel had the difficulty of habit in making the change as it was her own inability, in the first place, in the pronunciation of the name which brought about the use of Clover. She found it difficult, as she said, to get her tongue round Chloë. But she would try.

Hazel and Chloë, twin sisters, have a whole list of promises, agreements and disagreements between them. The Professor, being a twin himself, even if lacking now the childhood proximity to his twin, knows and understands the bond between his wife and her rather plain sister. He knows there is no such thing as an ugly woman, his own father told him this great truth and he has kept it as a remark to be passed on whenever he is in the position of accepted mentor.

Neither of the sisters could be described as pretty or even good-looking, rather they possess a particular energy and an unusual sense of humour which takes over from time to time. Hardly humour, he tells himself whenever he recollects, if he has to, one of their frolics. There was one night when Chloë was in the bed instead of Hazel. She appeared to be asleep. He knew at once it was Chloë. Sensitive to the slightest roughness on his own delicate skin, he has always known that Chloë was of a more prickly material than Hazel. Gallant, and holding within his heart the noble qualities of service and chivalry towards women and, at the same time, not wanting to spoil their innocent little joke, he switched off the bedside lamp as usual and, leaning over, he planted his goodnight kiss on the almost familiar bushy head of hair. He followed this with a small, hardly noticeable sexual movement towards her ... *Chloë*, so named, and in whom it might be possible to discover the exquisite, the unexpected, the pastoral delights of the romantically inclined shepherdess, beloved of Daphnis. And perhaps, as well, the possibility might even extend to the reaching of the famous yet tender green shoot, the cherished possession of Demeter herself, the goddess of the harvest and of fruitfulness.

Chloë, unsoftened by childbirth, was larger, heavier and even more solid than Hazel. As no erotic welcome was forthcoming he withdrew to his side of the bed to wait either for sleep or the morning, whichever should come first. But all this belongs to a time long past, when the three daughters were still mysterious bundles of wrapping cloths.

In subsequent balanced discussion they, the Professor, Hazel and Chloë, put this extreme playfulness down to the fact that they were all three under stress; in shock really, after the surprise of the multiple births. And they were, of course, housebound, confined like prisoners under house arrest, by the insatiable demands of the newcomers. The whole house was in disorder. The Professor, himself, was fortunate in that he escaped briefly every morning in order to deliver his nine a.m. lectures. These were sadly undistinguished, suffering from obscurity, since shortage of time caused them to be offered only in précis.

Over the years the Professor has developed the habit of retreating, without actually reading, into a literary work of his remembered choice. He is able to do this even when in the company of other people. He slips easily, while smiling at a little group of guests, into wishing for the experience of Flaubert's legendary cab drive, or that he could be like Robinson Crusoe, all alone on a desert island writing his diary and strolling along the beach to shoot a small goat for lunch.

He has come to understand that this is because he is wishing to be removed completely from his established place especially since Dr Florence is very much, and sweetly, on his mind. Flaubert's cab drive seems to claim every thought with the possibility of his being encapsulated and hidden within the confined space of a cab and moving at a tremendous pace, close to the passion-laden lips and subsequent kiss *and* the all-encompassing embrace, including the delicious little half-whispered *confidences of feeling* spoken with hesitation at first and then in little bursts of tenderness, with more confidence, being more eloquent and over-powering, as desire persists towards its more urgent and unrefusable stage. He, in his thoughts, attempts to put Dr Florence into a cab which resembles, in his imagination, Flaubert's horse-drawn, discreet convey-ance in which the travellers ride in complete seclusion. Theirs is a curtained privacy. The flight of the whipped horse takes them through one quiet street after another. The driver is seated on the box seat, whip whirling in readiness for the continuation of the wild journey, reckless in having no destination except that exquisite longed for moment which, ultimately, rewards the most urgent wish and desire.

Having taken Dr Florence like this into the wished for arms of love and complete seclusion, the Professor remembers that her clothes are tailored and severe, quite unlike the loose-flowing garments worn by Madame Bovary. He longs for simple muslin and soft lace which can be whispered and breathed aside as he approaches with reverence and suitable restraint keeping forever in mind Dr Florence's lack of experience and her complete innocence.

*I*n Cambridge once, years ago, someone said that his head resembled the beautiful drawing of Schiller, *Friedrich Schiller in 1780, zugeschrieben, Ölgemäde Weckherlin*. Schiller the writer of the famous 'Ode to Joy' (*Ode an die Freude*) and many other poems. The sensitive head, the drawing, was in the *Nationalmuseums* in Marbach and it was often suggested that he should go to Marbach to match his own aestheticism with that of the gentle poet. The Professor smiles when he recalls the remark. He always reminds himself that this was said often about many heads. He resumes his reading of an essay in which the writer has tried to bring literature, emotional needs, spiritual and psychological human development, social class, accepted rules and educational hopes all into one sentence. He looks up from the small neat handwriting, disturbed as usual.

He is disturbed by the soft rhythm of sound, the soft regular sound which accompanies the male pigeon's wooing of the female. The pigeons inhabit this side of the university, in particular the fourth-floor window-sills and a small balcony.

FOURTH FLOOR; DEPARTMENT OF ENGLISH. FOR MAIN OFFICE TURN LEFT. YOUR HEART THANKS YOU FOR USING THE STAIRS!

He sits in his chair, leaning back, pleasantly distracted and listening to the insistent persuasion. From his desk he can watch through his window and link the gentle but forceful vocal rhythm to the gentle rising and falling movements of the male bird's head together with the particular strutting walk, to and fro, along the shabby rusted gutters opposite.

During this repeated proud exercise the bird seems to increase in size as his breast feathers are ruffled and flushed up, displaying an ardent anticipation of passionate courtship.

Listening to the soft coaxing speech, the Professor

recalls easily the flutterings and shovings of these birds as they try at dusk, all of them together, to occupy for the night the same dirty window ledge high up, almost opposite his own window. There are several window ledges and there is no way of knowing why one particular one is so desirable. The Professor is often in his room at this particular time in the evening when students come by his open door hoping to be given an extension for a hopelessly late assignment, often offering an ancient medical certificate, an obsolete note from an exhausted and perhaps defeated practitioner.

He likes to be quietly in his room knowing that Dr Florence has a room in the same alcove, in the passage, and is probably there listening to the love song of the pigeons.

Shortly he will exchange his university study for his study at home where Hazel will bring the pinot noir and, perhaps, supply some music, something restful on cassettes. Some days, by invitation from Hazel, Dr Florence accompanies the Professor to take something which Hazel insists on calling 'pot luck with the family'.

*Elizabeth Jolley*

Sometimes, unexpectedly, the Professor remembers that once, years ago, he was walking across the fields, following Hazel and Chloë, he noticed then their short thick legs and the tender backs of their knees. At the time he resolved to remember, forever, the tenderness . . .

The change in the music always reminds the Professor of Dr Florence. There are many passages in music which recall Dr Florence. He does think about her often. It could easily be said that his mind is occupied with thoughts of Dr Florence, so much so that he experiences, sometimes, a small moment of physical excitement, a small thrill in the body brought about by the activity of the mind. Intrusive thoughts of his now grown-up daughters, returning for an important celebration, put an end for the time being to the intimate sweetness of his thoughts. It is something of a relief that his daughters are not yet on their return journey. In spite of this relief, he does love his daughters very much and would like them to know how much he has always loved them. The great test will be to see if they still accept this love, especially now, when returning after the freedom of travelling.

*And once sent out, a word takes wing beyond recall . . .*
And isn't this applicable to three small daughters who seemed, 'over night', to have become young women. Unfortunately there is no one present with whom the Horatian tag could be shared.

It is not impossible to recall his own father's unending gift of unconditional love. He understands now that to begin with, in order to avoid the anxiety of acceptance, he chose stupidity and easy memory. Always his mind was vacant, only occasionally filled with some meaningless, half-remembered childhood escapade, until one day, when he was a grown man but not yet of professorial status, he was walking with his father, they passed a café with little iron tables and ornamental chairs practically on the pavement. His father made the comment that, at one time, it was always women laughing and chatting with other women there in that place. Morning coffee, he said then, or light lunches. Now, he went on, he had noticed it is breakfasts.

And, sitting opposite each other, are men in pairs

in an embarrassing closeness, knees apart (possibly for intimate male reasons). Often a prematurely elderly man, plump, grey-headed and good-natured, is in some sort of control of the tete-a-tete (perhaps for having issued an invitation), but not quite, as it is a situation in which there is no prior knowledge, and which is entirely without any previous practical experience. The smooth complexion of the thinner and younger man is pale with a faint flush under the fine texture of his skin. This face can and does blush easily, revealing an inner, partly hidden pleasure and excitement, possibly the beginning of a confession or the special excitement which accompanies the realisation of a deeper under-standing, and promising an approach to more intimate knowledge with an amazement, never spoken about, of the self and of the inclinations of the other, offered with a completeness, the understanding of which cannot be denied. His father, as if surprised at himself, became silent.

The surprise of his father's unexpected observation, a sudden enlightenment, made a deep impression, widening in a dramatic moment, his own awareness and, at the same time, the recognition that his father, in his own right, because of his offering there in the street that morning, was never to be taken for granted or ignored.

And then there was Heraclitus, his father went on as if intent on clarifying, for his son's sake, the possibility and the nature of friendship, the most intimate and lasting friendship between men.

*They told me, Heraclitus*, he began to recite, *They told me you were dead*. It's a poem by a man called Cory, I think, it goes on like this:

> *They brought me bitter news to hear and bitter tears*
> *to shed*
> *I wept as I remembered how often you and I*
> *Had tired the sun with talking and sent him down the sky.*

'Then there was the Greek philosopher himself,' his father said after a pause. 'Five hundred and forty BC to 480, Heraclitus who is reported to have said that *everything flows and nothing stays* and that *it is not possible*

20

*to step in the same river twice.* You will know what is meant here.'

It is restful, the Professor admits to himself, to think of his father. His father, a little in awe of the rich well-bred accents, has always seemed fond of Hazel and Chloë as if grateful that his son is in capable hands.

'What are you reading now?' his father asked, changing the silence after his earlier remarks.

The Professor (who was neither Professor nor father then) explained that he was reading about Hippocrates, who, as well as being a physician famous for his recognition of the closeness of death in the changing appearance of the face of the dying individual, invented the Hippocratic Sleeve. It was made of cotton or linen or of a fine wool and was used for straining spiced wines.

'Hippocrates was well known for his wines.' His father surprised him even more with the information that the wines were frequently referred to by Chaucer.

Sitting quietly with a second and a third pinot noir, the Professor recalls that Hippocrates is mostly remembered for his observation that two pains in the body are better than one, as the stronger pain can obscure the lesser pain. Similarly a parallel exists in the emotional; and some sadness can benefit, can be lifted by an overcrowding of sorrows.

Memories of Hazel's mustard plasters together with her way of telling about a known disaster, in a sense, to dispel anything pressingly worrying, come to his mind as he allows his thoughts to drift.

He remembers the earlier days when the triplets were still 'in arms'. He went always to the super-market with Hazel. She had her list and the trolley and together they found the items in remembered places in the various aisles of the enormous store. It was a quick business-like visit, first thing on a Saturday morning. Other academics, Hazel would say, will be out early. So they would be even earlier and avoid the gossips who would hold them up with futile remarks. And then they would have to line up for ages at the checkout. Meanwhile the triplets, snug in lamb's wool in the car, might wake and be howling dreadfully, their little faces red, their heads rolling, their ineffectual tiny arms flailing and their little bodies arched and stiff with the effort of the prolonged howl.

It was during this time of the weekly joint shopping expeditions that the Professor discovered that he meant more than he realised to Dr Florence. It was after, immediately after, or really it was during a short walk, late at night, when he was seeing her home. He walked to the bus with her after dinner, saying he would like the walk, and she insisting that he need not come out and that she, flatly, would refuse to go home in the car because they were all so busy with the new triplets. The darlings! And the bus was quick and easy, stopping as it did, practically at her door.

The declaration was so nervously offered, her discovery within herself, her feelings, which she ought not to have, for him. She liked him so very much, much more than she ought to. In fact she couldn't help it, but she loved him.

He knows he will never forget the soft shy voice and her pale face, the honest expression in her eyes – her skin translucent in the pale light of a solitary street lamp by the bus shelter.

As she was speaking that night, he felt a great tenderness in his whole being for her. Deeply moved he, at once, took her smooth hand and held it to his lips gently. Putting a protective arm round her, he had then drawn her towards himself. Holding her close, he said that it would be a sweet idea for them, on such a fine night, to walk to her house together. He, with a light movement, stroked her soft hair. He felt her trembling against his body. She seemed to him then to be so very vulnerable. She had never shown herself as vulnerable till this moment. He wanted to stay with her all night so that she would not be alone. As they walked he told her that, though he was not able to give her all the love she ought to have, he was tremendously fond of her. He admired her, he told her. He did love her, he told her, she must know this, in a special sort of way he did love her. Her bus came by but he waved it on, and they continued to walk in that harmony which belongs to the giver and the recipient of the declaration from which there is no easy or rightful turning away.

The Professor, that evening, felt that on an occasion which demands chivalry, the person capable of it should be chivalrous. Though he had a tremendous desire to stay and to reward her love with an ardent caress and even some little display of passion, he understood that his own unmistakeable feelings should not be thought of first. This was a time really for reverence and tenderness towards Dr Florence. She should be made to feel protected and desirable and rewarded for giving expression to her feelings.

When they were at her front door he kissed her, making his kisses soft and sweet on her cheek and on her forehead, holding her closer during the little light kisses and telling her that they would be seeing each other soon. Every day they would be seeing each other. He promised to meet her the next day, the Saturday morning. He thought, he told her, that it would be sweet to see her in the fields at the back of the university. The newly mown hay would be fragrant and the barley, he thought it was still standing, would give them a private place in which to sit for a few minutes. He thought, he wanted to tell her, they could sit for a few precious minutes, silent in their awe.

He promised to meet her early on the Saturday morning, forgetting completely his well-worn and accustomed routine, until Hazel was bundling out through the kitchen door with the first instalment of triplets to the car.

Dr Florence, who was capable of asking a literary question which was both naïve and sexual, seemingly without understanding what was implied in her expression of curiosity, would just be leaving her house to keep their appointment – or was 'assignation' the more appropriate word? He was about to make an excuse to Hazel, as she was returning for the middle triplet, that there was a special meeting he could not miss, or that there was a new member of staff, a junior member . . . But he found he was completely unable to lie to Hazel especially as, of course, he was as responsible for the arrival of the triplets as she was and she, in all the bawling and the messiness of these strange, ugly, helpless, utterly selfish, little creatures, remained steadfastly cheerful and good-tempered, considering everything which had to be considered (and that included him) in the very full routine of the days and nights as they passed.

So there he was following Hazel's cheerful pouncings on jars of just the right jam (no time at all for the homemade jam which was her forté) and her spectacular grabbings for the specials of dried apricots and mineral water. He watched his *wife*, competent and unsuspecting, with her trolley, ahead of him, and allowed himself, while selecting from five different cat foods the one which their cat permitted herself to accept, a few moments to dwell on the new feelings which followed on from the sweetly shy, hesitant words spoken in the lowest of low voices. He had to realise that Dr Florence would be waiting, pale and shy, happy and unhappy in turn. She would be waiting for him, expecting him to appear, loving and kind, as if from some magic puff of the morning breeze or from a passing cloud. And, of course, he would not appear. She would wait and wait and be frail and wan with waiting. He could not help wondering which was worse, to be the anxious and tremulous one waiting, not knowing if the promise was made without any intention of it being kept, or whether it was even more unbearable to be caught as if trapped, unable to keep the appointment because of stacks of tomato-sauce bottles and pyramids of toilet rolls and the inescapable, impersonal curved glass counter housing, at eight-fifteen in the morning, dozens of golden stuffed and roasted chickens . . .

Hazel's solid back and her untidy (frizzed, the sisters called it) hair, no time at all now for the hair-dresser, and her absolute kindness and good-natured way of shopping began to irritate him as he longed to get away. He followed Hazel as she turned into the next aisle. She knew the method of the supermarket. She knew the sequence of the aisles, their numbers and the products they all contained. She often stopped and told other customers where they would find matches or rice or shampoo. She often reached for things for the elderly.

Fool that he was, it was more than likely that Hazel, who often described Dr Florence as being like one of the family, would have understood, without explanation from him, that he had agreed to see Dr Florence that morning. She would have accommodated the change in arrangements, asking Chloë to forgo her aerobics session, just this once, to 'jump in' with the big weekly shopping, leaving the Prof., as she often called him, to his tryst. Chloë, without changing from her purple tracksuit, would immediately have gathered her head scarf and the third triplet for its place in the car.

Chloë did her share in the household and never minded the tremendous extras which accompanied the arrival of the babies. They would all pull together, Chloë wisely remarked during a baffling first night with the newcomers. All three babies keeping up a serenade – or would it be called something else? A program of howling, perhaps. One after the other, as one was exhausted another took up the failing note with fresh strength and they, Chloë, Hazel and the Prof. himself, in an unexpected role, were pacing the floorboards, to and fro, all night.

In spite of an excellent mind and in spite of his handsome face and a particularly sweet smile, his *sweet good looks*, someone said once about the way in which his whole face lit up when he smiled, in spite of knowing this the Professor knows, as well, that at times he is almost craven in a despicable sort of way.

Perhaps, something, a certain shyness inherited from his mother (the Lady Delaware Carpenter), who seemed, throughout her life, to go out of her way to please people. She had not been able to thank Hazel (and Chloë) enough for taking her son off her hands. She admired the two sisters so much, she said so, often. It was their ability, she told him, their ability to draft the block bodice and then actually to be able to make a garment from this basic drawing. It was completely beyond her comprehension she insisted on telling him. And then there was their skill in memorising complicated knitting patterns after one swift and strenuous glance at the sacred hieroglyphics in someone else's magazine . . . in the doctor's waiting room . . .

However much he is thinking about Dr Florence and suffering now over her imagined tearful face, he is unable to see how he can possibly leave Hazel and Chloë with all the shopping, all the packets and bunches and jars and tins as well as the three babies who will be bellowing with indignation as they wait for their next nourishment.

What an idiot he was to make an arrangement with Dr Florence which he could not possibly keep.

Once before he had seen Dr Florence cry and he knew then, that because of her tears, in his presence, their position together was changed. He would always remember this side of her, the tears so near the surface. Once you saw someone cry, circumstances and possibly relationships were, forever, on a different level of feeling and importance. At the time he was explaining to Dr Florence that he understood completely why she wanted a sympathetic reading and a suitable qualification, a good grade, she said then, for Ms Bianca's Dissertation. He noticed the use of the word 'grade' and felt that it had come straight from Ms Bianca herself. Plainly the work was hardly an academic literary discussion, a thesis; and not wanting to say this he became reserved, breaking off his discourse and then, while Dr Florence wept, he fell into one of his Cambridge silences.

As he recalls the scene now, he tries to find an explanation. It seems suddenly, in the stress of the shopping and the thought of Dr Florence waiting endlessly for him, that the friendship between the two women might be deeper than he realised previously. His question, unasked of course, except within his own thoughts, is whether in trying not to be 'too fond', her phrase, of him, Dr Florence is consoling herself in being consoled by Ms Bianca. He wonders if Ms Bianca is capable of real feelings for Dr Florence. And he wonders seriously if he has, in some way, caused the two women to deepen their friendship. He has always held the thought, without applying it specifically, that women would be adept at knowing exactly, for themselves and each other, the ways in which consolation would be the more exquisite. His feeling of jealousy is suddenly heightened. Mixed with these feelings is a sense of intrigue and curiosity. He tries to imagine the bedroom in the apartment house which they share, he thinks, as lovers. It is not difficult to imagine the white and gold furniture, the little decorations of porcelain, the magazines, the scattered underclothes, the raided dressing-table top and, for the walls, some pictures; someone's cornfields in colour (prints), and the well-known *Smiling Woman* of

Augustus John. The bedroom, a secret little nest for lovers, an apartment for two, quite unlike Hazel's bedroom which, of course, he shares, and which is never private.

In the car with the three babies silent, red-faced and subdued in their lamb's wool, and the smooth movement of Hazel's excellent handling of the car, he recalls easily now, that he sat shrouded in his own thoughts. It seemed impossible to think, then, that he, a kind and honest man, had thrown Dr Florence and Ms Bianca together. He remembers that he smiled, half-hidden in shopping bags, at his conceited and self-important thought. Dr Florence and that woman, Ms Bianca, for heaven's sake! Her real name is Shirley, Shirley something or other . . .

Dr Florence herself, with her long soft brown hair, so like his own, and her large brown eyes, comes from a distinguished family and background. On her desk, in the department, she has a photograph of her father, a portrait in oils of him in uniform, something European and, for the painting, casual. He is sitting, with a benevolent but serious expression, on the corner of his massive desk, his hands crossed in leisure over the area where his genitals are, inside the military dress, in repose.

The Professor has often brooded on the fact that Dr Florence, without being able to help it, looks and behaves as if she has come from an aristocratic stem. A purity established long ago, years of good breeding, good manners and high ideals which would remain, forever, in evidence in the slender delicate bone structure and the enviable gracefulness of her whole being. She is tall, taller than Hazel and taller than Chloë who, while being well born and cultured, are from a different background in human breeding. Both Hazel and Chloë are terrifically good sports. They would never indulge in unkind gossip and they would never knowingly cheat anyone. It is likely that they would both be deeply shocked if they could know the Professor's secret thoughts. Hazel and Chloë who both, before travelling to Australia, played hockey for England, are not delicately made.

Dr Florence, with her extra height, has no extra flesh. Her breastbone is evident, well defined, and her breasts are small. Her body is fashioned with such exquisite good taste that it is possible to imagine how acutely she would feel, experience is a better word, every sensation. She is not buried, the Professor tells himself it is a figure of speech, she is not buried in extra fat or muscle and her fine skin is like silk, being almost transparent.

When the Professor compares the two women he feels ashamed of his critical approach to Ms Bianca who seems to him to be rather vulgar in her use of language, her head movements, her self-assured manner and in the handling of knives and forks, cups and saucers and table napkins. He knows that people are often attracted towards each other when it would seem unlikely. This was one of the inexplicable things about the subject. In his private thoughts, not shared with anyone, he sometimes has doubts about himself. He speculates on other married couples, academics mainly because he is not acquainted with other sorts. He likes, rather too much perhaps, seeing the young girls on graduation nights. He likes to see them, slender and eager, coming up, one after the other, to receive their certificates. He admires their youthful, smooth, creamy complexions and the ridiculous and rather touching tiny articles of clothing protesting beneath the newly acquired academic gowns.

The thin ankles and very small feet of the slim young man, the university organist, fascinate him. Whenever he is able to watch the nimble and dedicated movements of this man, he realises that he has never seen his face. He had no idea, till he saw this man playing the organ that the instrument is played with the whole body. Intimate and scholarly, dramatic and tender. Completely absorbing.

The Professor reminds himself, he understands, that he has never seen the organist's face.

He understands, the Professor understands, he told Dr Florence that day when she cried in his study at the university. He understands, he explained, that she wants to do something kind for Ms Bianca. He, lowering his voice, explained then, carefully, that a 'Masters' simply cannot be given to anyone simply because we happen to know the candidate and have a special relationship with her. We must never, he told

her, be unethical. We must keep to highly moral stan-
dards, he told her.

By this time it is both an aggravation and a
comfort to consider the passing of some hours and the
fact that probably Dr Florence is now in the arms of
her lover Ms Bianca; Shirley Something. He has read
about the theory of the perfection of the same-sex
orgasm. In his consideration he can imagine a privileged and well-educated man being drawn towards an
illiterate opposite or perhaps not exactly illiterate, but
someone not so thoroughly well read. And since the
attraction does not require similar backgrounds and
similar academic interests it might be possible, in imagination, to reach an understanding, physical, with a
labourer of some sort, a mechanic or a shop assistant.

He has to consider, as well, the hundred per cent
expectation of rewarding satisfaction for both partici-
pants. He thinks once more of Dr Florence and Ms
Bianca and feels excluded.

The rod and the spray of the shower droop. The Professor, shy in his nakedness in a strange bathroom, has to crouch. He fumbles for the soap. As it slips between his searching fingers he wishes the conference was over and that he could be on his way home, sipping a well-named, suitably chilled, white wine and reading a stupid novel. He would be pleasantly half asleep, he thinks, lulled by the noise of the plane and the presence of an elderly colleague, familiar and undemanding, in the seat beside his.

It is never easy, he knows, to adjust the hot water in a different place. He shivers under the tepid sprinkling and is shocked a few minutes later at his own unattractive appearance; the ruthless mirrors offering hitherto unknown aspects of his body. Inexperience causes some delay in finding the bath towels. Forgetful, having unpacked some things and not others, afraid of being late, he dresses in a hurry. He thinks someone is entering the room but it is merely his own reflection in yet another mirror, full-length, on the inside of the door.

There is too an ever present feeling that his room is on the ground floor though it is, in fact, on the twenty-ninth. The room has the solid appearance of being on the ground floor. The walls above the dark panelling of polished wood are a rich olive green. There are deep window seats and an enormous writing desk of the same dark polished wood. The desk is covered with tooled leather and there are soft leather folders arranged on it. A thorough determination towards good taste is evident in the five substantial leather armchairs and the picture frames, which are ornamental, containing paintings of flowers and restful landscapes. The lamps, five in all, are of polished brass. He supposes there is television, discreetly hidden. The room gives the impression that it has been designed to welcome a male guest.

He has slept well but lacks the expected refresh-ment of sleep. This morning his head cold reaches its zenith with fourteen earth-shattering sneezes; a sort of sonnet in fourteen harrowing lines containing in their shortness the necessary touch of philosophy. As he tells himself later, the sneezes are an indication that he is, to use one of his wife's phrases, on the mend.

Haunted now by the memory of his ordered breakfast the day before, he leaves with cautious steps and backward glancings and, closing his door carefully, he approaches the elevators. He wishes, during the rapid journey downward to what he hopes will be a simple breakfast, that he had not made the strange arrangement for later on in the evening. He thinks of it, with some apprehension, as an appointment with the flesh.

There are many difficulties connected with long-distance travelling and involvement with conferences. One of these difficulties is indecision. Normally able to make up his mind about something quite quickly, he wastes time wondering which tie to wear with which shirt and whether to order room service or to go down to the hotel dining room. He is ashamed to admit to himself that he wastes energy on such trivial matters. He supposes it is because he is removed from the familiar. His desk at home in his study, and his desk in his office in the university, and bookshelves in both places enable him to pass easily through any moments of inactivity. There is nothing in the expensive elaborate folders on the hotel-room desk to satisfy his restless prowlings. As for his own slim folder, prepared for the conference, it would not do to glance through this. A last-minute fit of indecision would cause him to feel he should completely rethink and rewrite his lecture before the afternoon, and this would mean telephoning Hazel, long-distance, for notes and references for an entirely different presentation.

It is during these short but seemingly endless times between conference meals and events that his mind descends towards a depth of uneasiness which borders on depression.

Alone in his room once more the Professor stands as close to the window as the deep ledge will allow. Not able to bear looking down to the street below, he stares at the different levels of the rooftops. All are covered with stains and ugly rough patches. Some are littered with coils of old rope and wire. Others are piled with rusty metal boxes and containers, perhaps mysterious para-phernalia for maintenance. People inside the buildings cannot know what reposes above their ceilings. In one direction he can see trees and a small park. In another, there is a pattern of railway lines disappearing towards a distant horizon which might contain mountains, rivers, the ocean, other cities, other universities, other hotels.

Yesterday, his first morning in the hotel, his dish of prunes and a serving of bacon and eggs was brought to his room on a trolley draped with spotless white tablecloths. It was decorated with fresh flowers, fruit and champagne. The young waiter proudly showed him the hot oven within the trolley, a massive dish of bacon and eggs, sausages, chops, mushrooms and fried toma-toes. The bakery basket contained rolls, wholemeal and white, croissants, muffins and toast. There was, as well, a plate with butter, jam and honey. The dish of prunes would have supplied a whole family. The Professor, greatly embarrassed, waited while the young waiter explained the breakfast and exploded the champagne. He is still embarrassed and would like to forget the experience.

He paces across the clean wasteland of carpet and goes once more into the small private bathroom to take a last critical look at himself in the bright light. It seems, all at once, that his large, slightly hooked nose is fleshier, even rather coarse. He supposes this is the result of advancing years and frequent glasses of wine. He wonders if the great philosophers, in the past, worried about their noses.

A gastric uneasiness, which often accompanies him when travelling, is worse this time especially when he contemplates the extraordinary request and the agreement. An agreement given all too rapidly. He supposes he was flattered. He thinks of his wife. Though she was present during the particular conversation, at this moment she seems remote. It is as if he is unable to think of her name, as if the request from the two women in his department has intruded. All he can recall now is the automatic way in which she, his wife Hazel, unfolded some cream-coloured, fine woollen material and, after some silent mental calculations, set about sketching little patterns on clean transparent paper which she, with deft movements, pinned to the cloth in readiness for the special work of cutting out.

She had the cloth by her, she explained, as she took out her dressmaking scissors. She had the cloth by her, he remembers everything she said on that afternoon. There was very little discussion, it being thought that further talk could continue when Dr Florence and Ms Bianca and the Professor, himself, were all in the same hotel attending the same conference.

Dr Florence and Ms Bianca are frequent visitors. In the department friendships grow and blossom. They die and grow again in different directions. But Dr Florence and Ms Bianca have been sharing an apartment and a small car for some time and are regarded by others as being a couple (and not simply for economic reasons). One is never invited without the other and both entertain visitors, that sort of thing; they entertain visitors together. They often ask if they can visit the Professor and Hazel. Hazel, in her jovial way, says of course they can come Sunday afternoons and help wash the family car or weed the front garden, these being Hazel's things to do on Sundays.

She had the cloth by her, Hazel told them more than once. And he has in his mind, forever, the image of her perseverance with her self-imposed, almost automatic task. He seems, even now, to hear her quick intake of breath as she smooths and folds and cuts, wielding the scissors with a kind of grace, neatly rounding small curves and nipping delicately at what she calls the notches.

It never ceases to amaze him, even after many years, his wife's accuracy in cutting out. A well-made garment depends very much on the way in which it is cut out in the first place. And he knows that there is no way in which, if the cutting out is badly done, it can be put right later.

It gives him pleasure to think of this as a possible metaphor for use in a lecture. Certainly it is applicable to the paper he is to deliver at the end of the afternoon.

His title, or topic is a better word, 'Conscious and Conscience'. His theme being that the human individual is conscious from birth but conscience has to be developed by example, by cherishing and by teaching. And then, later, by experience and challenge and the awareness brought about by the quiet and unseen drama of internal rite of passage. And who can do this, he will question, who can do this more satisfactorily than the writers of poetry, drama and fiction? He has, in his lecture notes, examples from Thomas Traherne and John Wilmot, Earl of Rochester, in the seventeenth century, to the poets of the present time.

Depending on his audience (he is always careful not to offend conference visitors, for example, a group of kindly middle-aged English teachers or a handful of nuns from a teaching order), he sometimes describes Rochester's terrible death, a punishment in itself; *an ulcer in the bladder is broken and he pisses matter, he is in extreme pain*: described in a letter, June 1680, from Gilbert Burnet to the Earl of Halifax; and sometimes he leaves out the report concentrating on the development of conscience mentioned in the same letter wherein Burnet writes that he, Lord Rochester, *after a life of debauchery has expressed great remorse for his past life* and *dies a serious penitent professing himself to be a Christian.*

The precise use of the cutting-out scissors can be seen as a metaphor for the early and correct shaping of the child before he becomes the man. The metaphor becomes even more significant if the garments being shaped are simple little gowns for an expected baby.

The Professor is disturbed by the request and the meeting which is to follow later this evening. Especially this is because of a coincidence, his intention to refer pleasantly and somewhat lightheartedly, during delivery, to the 'happy minute', the 'little death' that restores, perhaps renews is a better word, life and happiness. The wonderful feeling of calm, the peace after orgasm, the 'little death', this traditional joke which has attracted poets over the centuries. He contemplates having to leave, unmentioned, references of this sort in view of the presence of Dr Florence and Ms Bianca and their expectations.

There has not been an opportunity for private discussion with Dr Florence. Always now, as if to claim as well as to protect, Ms Bianca is forever present, assertive and vocal. He supposes that this must be 'for the best' in the circumstances. It has been made clear that if they do carry out their plan, the Prof. must be prepared to 'do his share'. Ms Bianca has been both coy and loud.

Ms Bianca has insisted, in various conversations, on 'the natural way'; and Dr Florence, with a small shrug, seems in the softest voice, to have murmured 'whatever' as if it was 'all one' to her. The Professor himself, having recognised a change taking place, has been made to understand that his 'goodnight' kisses, in the hedge, will continue to be restrained, because they have to be, as if from a kindly but uninvolved relative and completely without desire. The whole undertaking being 'a means to an end'.

When he was preparing his paper earlier he had some understanding of the idea being cherished by both Dr Florence and Ms Bianca. He would prefer to keep the reference, if it would not emotionally disturb

Dr Florence, to the 'little death' in his lecture. He thinks of it as something very tender in life and in poetry. It is not always attainable. It is something to laugh over lovingly in secret, a private joke for lovers and a time, too, for the gentle laughter of consolation and future promise in the face of failure.

The Professor, sitting through the morning sessions of the conference, is making small neat notes in the margins of his pages. He likes to make flattering reference, when it is his turn, to the earlier speakers. He has to confess, somewhere inside himself, that his thoughts are wandering from the earnest deliveries, these being mostly from young academics with too much prepared material. His own paper is to be something of an intellectual entertaining reward for everyone at the end of the long day. He glances quickly at the rows on either side of him but is not able to see Dr Florence or her friend Ms Bianca. Aware of his own inattention he tries to look as if he is listening but his thoughts are, in a personal way, directed towards the wish to be entirely alone with

Dr Florence after the delivery of his lecture. He tries to think of other things.

He often wonders if he resembles his predecessor. The two men never met. Chiefly, he has always suspected, this was because of the university's policy, 'penchant' might be a better word (he easily imagines the indiscreet salivation at the boardroom table) for saving money; the new head of department, himself in this instance, not being appointed until a year after the retirement of the previous head. The outcome is, of course, that the members of the department, accustomed to being without a head, take very little notice of him in departmental matters. He is not clear whether this is because of a carefree, happy, unsupervised year or whether it is, in fact, a reflection on the attitudes and the ways of this other man. He is not able to remember now the other man's name.

Often vague thoughts cross his mind between lines of poetry which come to him, unbidden, at surprisingly frequent intervals. One particular thought is that, in the eyes of the department, he is of no consequence. He is hopeless, he knows, over money matters and is secretly grateful that others in the department know exactly what their funding is and how 'to keep this rolling' (their phrase).

Feeling restless he leaves his place in the auditorium and goes to a side door which is marked as a way out. As two speakers are exchanging places at the lectern, his leaving will not be noticed. It is half-past twelve and his turn is not until four forty-five. Plenty of time for a short walk and for ambivalent thoughts about his prepared discourse.

Outside the side door there is a smooth path, between well-kept lawns and flower beds, leading to an artificial lake which has a bridge over the narrow end. The Professor, breathing in the fragrance of grass and water, feels refreshed.

> *As Chloris full of harmless thought*
> *Beneath the willows lay . . .*

He thinks of the poets long ago who were inspired to write from rural scenes, even though this one is contrived and artificial. He pauses on the little bridge and looks across the rippling patterns of light and shade on the surface of the water. The willow trees on the opposite bank, trailing their long thin wands and leaves in the lake, bring a continuation of the poem to his mind:

> *As Chloris full of harmless thought*
> *Beneath the willows lay*
> *Kind love a comely shepherd brought*
> *To pass the time away.*

The Professor during desultory and nervous revisings of his lecture interrupts these thoughts and thinks instead about Dr Florence and Ms Bianca and their intimate wish:

> *The finest plans have always been spoiled by the littleness*
> *of them that should carry them out. Even Emperors cannot*
> *do it all by themselves.*

That Dr Florence could only approach the subject with this quotation was clearly an indication that delicacy would be needed, at that time, in the ensuing conversation.

From his place on the ornamental little bridge he can see the spread of water over the grass and is reminded momentarily of the demented streams in his childhood. They, the boys, often walked from the school to fields nearby where the floodwater, spreading over the grass, shone in the sunlight and they, as one man, felt at once forced to pull off their school boots and socks and to walk with unaccustomed gentleness on this grass, temporarily submerged and soft and mysterious, beneath the escaped and sparkling water.

In the peaceful surroundings he considers yet again his favourite seventeenth-century poets; especially the poet Traherne and his poem celebrating birth:

*Such Sacred Treasures are the Lims in Boys*
*In which a Soul doth Dwell;*
*Their organized Joynts, and Azure Veins*
*More wealth include, than all the World contains . . .*

These lines remind him that in the wishful suggestion concerning the fulfilling of a certain aspect in their lives and their relationship, the two women might have over-looked the necessary accompanying feelings of love and respect. The act required of him needs that special love which embraces every detail of the two people and the life they hope to share. It is a love which promotes noble thoughts and clever ideas and is contained in the warmth of complete trust, the trust which lasts forever.

The soft grassy roundness of the bank beneath the willows opposite offers him a few moments of reflection on that particular small mound which sweetly invites and cushions the male approach:

> *It is the workhouse of the World's great trade;*
> *On this soft anvil all mankind was made.*

He would like to surprise, with gentleness, both women, Dr Florence more especially, with the thoughtful words at exactly the time of his approach. He will be elated, in the presence of the women, after the successful delivery of his paper and the glasses of champagne which are to follow the final session of the conference. It is doubtful that either Dr Florence or Ms Bianca will be familiar with the particular lines from the poet, the infamous rake, Wilmot, Earl of Rochester.

He is, he thinks, like Teiresias. For though predominantly male in tone of voice, in build and demeanour, in dress, in outward appearance and in certain outward pleasures, reading and lecturing and other pastimes regarded as pleasing to a man, he does seem able to inhabit completely a woman's experience and her ability to be thoughtful and kind. He prides himself on having the special attributes which accompany the tender and the affectionate in the way of recognising the shiver of ecstasy when the mind bows down in homage before beauty. He knows he has been careless at times. But, like Teiresias, while making various pronouncements and at least one serious judgment on human life, he has always acknowledged that 'No man alive is free from error'.

Continuing with his examination of human existence, the Professor, following the teaching of Socrates,
who declared that the unexamined life is not worth
living, investigates in every thought and feeling his
own extra sensitivity as it transcends all experience of
both man and woman; but without boasting as Teiresias himself boasted. Simply the Professor, with quiet
assurance, accepts this exquisitely complete erotic and
aesthetic gift. Often when he is having these thoughts
it is as if he is holding Dr Florence in an embrace so
passionate and tender he has to calm himself by
controlling his thoughts to something ordinary. The
Professor smiles as he recalls Hazel's advice to anyone
making a salad: 'Always remember to allow one lettuce
leaf per person.'

Thinking of Hazel brings another thought, a
disturbing thought. There are now three people in the
proposal instead of two. If Hazel is actually included
(and she has in her own way included herself) – he
lets his thoughts gallop like a horse without its rider:
Hazel, Hazel-nut, the ancient celtic fruit of wisdom,
Hazel the wise, Hazel his wife, with her prompt attack

on the creamy material – if she is included she brings the number to four people being directly involved. Her matter-of-fact, practical approach is so different from his posy-strewn path; all the same, if an honest view is taken, it has to be understood that the whole exercise has to be looked upon with an acceptance of the result. Hazel's approach, with her cutting-out scissors, provides this acceptance. And once she is busy with her treadle sewing machine the three of them, the Professor, Dr Florence and Ms Bianca, know that they are being left to amuse themselves, perhaps with theatre or concert tickets or an evening walk returning to the apartment house shared by Dr Florence and Ms Bianca, where, in the moonlight, the Professor (almost as part of the hedge) will press himself close to each woman, first one and then the other, bestowing professorial, affectionate goodnight kisses, and keeping his thoughts and actions simply on this level.

An excitement, a sense of importance and a feeling of tenderness and wisdom, all these envelop him as he allows himself to consider in detail, but with respect, the more youthful and possibly attractive bodies of both Dr Florence and Ms Bianca. That they want a child to bring up together is natural. He is prepared to consider and understand Hazel's reasoning which, at the time, comes as a surprise to all of them, Hazel included. She, straightening up from the cutting out, is prepared to consider the suggestion that each of the two women may want the experience. Both women should have the chance to be pregnant and to give birth to a child. Two babies, in Hazel's reasoning, would be more beneficial than one. (After all, she has enough material for a dozen little gowns.) Two babies, siblings, growing up together, and both women simultaneously being fulfilled with motherhood.

Dr Florence and Ms Bianca, having had thoughts about one child only, seem at once fully prepared to accept this new thought. The Professor, seeing the ease with which a new idea is understood and approved, congratulates, in silence, the excellent tutorial system nurtured within the department.

Dr Florence and Ms Bianca explain once more

that they want an intellectual father for their children. Apart from what they persist in describing as his 'fine brain', he is very handsome. They become, during the afternoon, more excited, saying that he has beautiful hands and eyes. Especially his hands which they insist can be compared favourably with Lytton Strachey's hands in Dora Carrington's famous 1916 portrait. He does not need to be told this, they are sure, but they are telling him all the same; they tell him that afternoon over Hazel's willow-pattern teacups and her rock cakes, they want him to know. Also they explain that his daughters (his and Hazel's, of course) are lovely girls. A wonderful pattern, 'example' would be a better word, ahead of them for their own expectations. Hazel, acknowledging the compliment, adds the wise remark that Dr Florence and Ms Bianca can take it in turns to go to work, a sort of rostered arrangement, she says.

The Professor, resting on the little bridge with both hands on the smooth railing, closes his eyes and enjoys from memory the window in his study at home. This window is tall and narrow, filled from outside with green foliage. The white lace curtains, always freshly washed, stirred by the light breeze, float and swell, moving lightly inwards and outwards. This pleasant image is accompanied by thoughts of his three daughters, a whole bunch of babies, a multiple birth, unexpected yet expected, for Hazel and her sister, Chloë, are twins and he is a twin himself. His daughters, they purse their pretty mouths and pout. They use lipstick with names like 'Anger' and 'Lust' and they discuss at the dinner table the merits of the different deodorants and tampons advertised on television.

The girls, he has several cherished images of them. They were born within minutes of each other and are now at boarding school. During holidays, when there are dinner guests, these daughters move with grace between the substantial armchairs, handing little squares of pink and yellow Turkish delight, followed by tiny cups of black coffee, to the assembled visitors. In their simple white (princess-style) dresses made by their mother and the little shawls of soft grey wool, knitted by their aunt Chloë, they are gentle enough to have stepped straight from a Jane Austen novel into Hazel's unplanned and rather shabby room.

The Professor, whenever he goes away, even while still at the airport before the outward journey, wishes to be at home. Trying to dismiss the cosy pictures of peaceful family life, he walks on across the little bridge as if to leave the ever present complication of homesickness and other thoughts hovering just above the innocent water.

The well-kept lawns, during vacation, are smooth and empty of students. He wants to thank someone for the open air and the pensive sky during these minutes of freedom away from the packed hours of the conference weekend. He recalls with quiet excitement, from previous visits, that the path leads on into the wild edges of the bush. There are remembered narrow paths leading through the fragrant wilderness, a curious mixture of fallen eucalyptus trees with foliage still sprouting and often with plants growing from beneath dead branches and burned undergrowth. Hazel, if walking with him, would look with disapproval at the surroundings, declaring that a good raking out and burning was needed. Hazel is the only person he knows who can study the state of the ground and, at the same time, pay homage to the circling flight of a wedge-tailed eagle, a golden predator, the only creature able to look directly at the sun, high up in the clear blue sky above a clearing in the forest. Hazel with her practical good sense in housekeeping and sewing, in gardening and with knowledge about birds has absolutely no feelings of envy or jealousy. She is never mean or bitter.

The Professor knows his own weakness, he enjoys penetrating young women with a handsome glance. He knows too that the glance is not always purely intellectual even though it comes from the excitement of sudden understanding. He delights in conversations in which he explains with superb literary references and a scholarly precision, reaching across centuries, that relationships of different kinds are acceptable if approached and conducted with civilised dignity. He is known to break off in the middle of a lecture earnestly requesting the students to name, from the floor, the most important aspects of the personality. He interrupts immediately the beginnings of a single shy response to tell the massed faces in the auditorium, yes! yes! they are right; love and complete trust are the greatest and the most important of the characteristic human attributes.

He thinks now, during his stolen walk, of Dr Florence and the conversation during the visit on the afternoon before they, Dr Florence, Ms Bianca and he, himself, left for the conference.

Dr Florence, a valuable member of his department, is no longer young but obviously is not post-menopausal, though she must be near enough and would need a competent reliable obstetrician, none of this 'natural childbirth in a corner of a field' talked about so cheerfully by Ms Bianca.

Dr Florence, Florentius and Florentia, the derivation is from the Latin *florens*, he thinks, which means flowering. He smiles. Dr Florence should have her flowering *and* her deflowering.

Dr Florence, 'Florence' is unusual for a surname. Her Christian or given name is quite ordinary, he remembers, Betty or something like that . . .

Dr Florence is the only person he knows, to have parked her car on the rough grass alongside the freeway, an enormous road, the only one going east. She wants to walk there in that alien ugly place, she explains, when asked. She wants to be familiar with the verges should her own car break down in that uninhabited place where, on both sides, there are stretches of sand and coarse grass, the territory of starving hawks and certain derelict men employed in the particular, and not unimportant, light industry wherein starved cattle bodies are reduced in cauldrons in the processing and packaging of pet foods. Whenever the Professor thinks about this, he thinks he can smell the scorched hides and the charred bones. Dr Florence is the only person he knows, who makes the fearsome right-hand turn at the first wide intersection, in order to follow a painted cardboard notice announcing that roses are growing and hidden somewhere in that barren place. She has described in detail, for him, the old-fashioned rose garden, a small nursery packed with plants and flowers, bedded between tiny green hedges, and fenced with old pickets, overgrown and supported by bindweed and honeysuckle. A well-watered plot, she explains, a safe nest, a cradle perhaps, for cultivation and propagation.

Whatever he thinks of the sweet description which Dr Florence gives of this fragrant and pretty place, he wishes that he could gather her up and take her in his arms to this garden of seclusion and innocence. He wants to admire her nakedness and to reward her wishes of love. As he thinks, his desire becomes more intense. He allows himself to recall her appearance and every word of her timid declaration. He holds in his heart the thoughts of the walk they had in the night and, even more, he remembers the walk home by himself; so full of tender thoughts he was, that the distance was covered without his noticing.

And now ahead of him is the strange but under-standable request. Fathering babies. Apparently permissible. No eyebrows were raised. That is to say, Hazel and Chloë did not raise theirs.

The late evening 'appointment' has serious disadvantages. There is no possibility of a handsome performance at dawn should there be a failure (his, of course) at midnight.

'To become immortal and then die,' the Professor hears his own voice with some surprise. He is alone in the silence and his voice sounds like the voice of someone old, tentative and even questioning. He has been walking for some time. He listens to the dry twigs cracking beneath his feet. It is time to turn back.

Thinking of Dr Florence he has to acknowledge over again that Ms Bianca is quite a different sort of person. Ms Bianca, in his opinion, is simply one of the many bright but uneducated women pouring into English departments all over the country, taking degrees, many of them, he thinks, without any sense of real scholarship. He is not against this, they are, he tells Hazel from time to time, they are admirable women. There is absolutely nothing wrong in seeking enrichment. But he fails to understand how Dr Florence and Ms Bianca can sustain this friendship which they clearly mean to have on an intimate and permanent basis. Children, he knows, do not necessarily hold two people together, and there are times when children drive a wedge between a man and wife. He tries often to understand how Dr Florence can need this woman, a woman who flirts (a strong word but he is not exaggerating) with everyone, male and female. Perhaps strangely enough, with women, though Hazel remains completely unaware of the eyelids fluttering in her direction.

He has heard Dr Florence, after being asked with a false shyness, painstakingly explaining in the lecture hall, a metaphor which has a strong sexual meaning, when he himself has explained the same one to the same questioner, Ms Bianca, in the classroom the previous day. If comparisons are to be made, she is dishonest in the presence of Hazel's solid honesty. Hazel is always simply Hazel and never tries to be anything she is not. He finds this very boring but, at the same time, restful.

Straight after giving birth (multiple), almost before the baby girls had finished their first howlings, Hazel asked for her wellingtons. Apparently she had been setting out some small cabbages during the onset of labour, and wanted to finish the planting before nightfall.

'Hazel has both feet on the ground.' His mother-in-law, on that occasion, had made the suitable remark which she immediately improved upon by adding, 'I should say *in* the ground.' This same mother-in-law, with her high-pitched pealing laugh, had said at the wedding to her son-in-law, the Professor, that if anything happened to Hazel there was always Chloë. Chloë, the sister, being a twin, an exact replica, even to the tendency toward hairiness and a down on the upper lip (almost a moustache) of Hazel.

There is in his own family and his marriage an inheritance of good health. Hazel's mother declares often that hairy legs and arms are a sign of strength in the human individual. The Professor is aware of his own lack of body hair at such times. He hopes that he is not, with the arrangement ahead of him, open to infection.

Often during a lecture he pauses to recite in Middle English a passage from *The Canterbury Tales* (The Prologue). He knows his voice is measured and melodious, tender at times, with little inflexions of irony. He enjoys hearing his own voice. He goes on, sometimes, to explain to his audience that in Chaucer's time venereal infections were chronic and somewhat low-key, being present in most people. As people, he explains, as people during the ages became cleaner in their personal habits, bacteria were forced to become more virulent, thus making the infection more persistent and more savage. After a significant short pause he continues with another recitation, still in the Middle English this time from 'The Nun's Priest's Tale'. He goes over time with these recitations, not noticing that a number of the students are slipping out sideways on bent legs, their shoulders hunched and their faces hidden by their hair.

Being a little out of breath with his walking, he supposes now that he no longer looks youthful. Should he, for example, with appropriate flowers, magazines and chocolates visit the new mothers (when the time comes), a cheerful young nurse would be sure to greet him, calling out, 'Hello Grandpa, second door down the passage on the left.' Without thinking at all, he realises he has presumed that Dr Florence and Ms Bianca will be postnatal simultaneously and naturally will want to share their hospital room.

The Professor does not feel old, not at all. He knows he is slender and gentle. People, women have told him this. One woman at a university party even said, that, to her, he resembled the graceful young Goethe in the 1782 Tischbein painting, *Goethe in the Roman Campagna*. In spite of this compliment he is inclined to wish for a more substantial Germanic stance or, failing that, the cold, blue-eyed, thick shape of Ibsen. In spite of his melancholy brown eyes and the soft brown hair curling behind his ears, he likes the idea of the solid professorial presence. He likes to approach his house. He cultivates the dignified walk up the path. He takes care to pause before selecting his key and inserting it in the lock of the front door. He opens the door with the little flourish of owner-ship. There is, too, a hint that some trick of magic has just been carried out, and he steps into his entrance hall, the successful conjurer.

The little bow which accompanies the insertion of the key and the opening of the door is all a part of the restrained power of the Lover and is one of his developed consolations. Over the years he has developed, 'created' is perhaps a better word, a series of consoling images and thoughts. Promising himself a poet's hat and a short cloak of some rough, woollen cloth, an Austrian Loden perhaps, he has smiled at reproductions of the young Goethe. Another consolation of a more realistic sort is remembering the well-brushed long hair of his three daughters. They all have a delightful way of glancing up quickly, with a little smile of shy expectation, when they are spoken to by their mother or a visitor. The hope and innocence in their faces give him pleasure as he recalls their expressions but, at the same time, imagined fears for their future take hold of him and he, all at once, feels short of breath as if he had some insidious illness hidden inside him.

He breathes in the warm sweet fragrance of the vegetation. He is sure he can smell honey. Possibly one of the tall trees has an immense store of honey within. He has read of such things.

He thinks, with pleasure as he walks, of his forthcoming lecture. A lecture for him is like a musical performance. He has his opening phrase, his first sentence like an instrument, solo, and then with careful orchestration he brings in one point after another, little headings which will be repeated and enlarged upon during his discourse.

Part of the pleasure of giving a lecture lies in the intense moments before he enters the crowded lecture hall. Ahead of him is the sound, the rising and falling sound of many voices. The sound rises and falls and rises again, and then there is the complete silence when he enters and hears his own footsteps crossing to the lectern. This has been prepared for him with a special bright light which will shine directly on to his pages. And to one side there is a sparkling glass of cold water.

But first there is his greeting, which comes easily and pleasantly with an amusing aside sending a subdued ripple of pleased anticipation through his audience.

He is looking forward to his lecture. He loves to lecture. He starts easily, his voice rising and falling. Pausing, he looks along the rows of faces and, with a gentle thrust, he asks a question. He pauses and then answers the question at once with special sustained emphasis. And, to his immediate satisfaction, he sees heads bending forward as notes are scribbled on pages in the folders of various colours which students seem to carry everywhere. Sometimes he will invite a student up to the lectern to read aloud a certain paragraph in a text, or perhaps two students to read a dialogue. He likes the idea that he is conducting or producing a performance. For this particular evening he has asked for a semicircle of six chairs and an additional microphone in order for six people from the audience to take part in a spontaneous discussion beginning with a statement on the meaning of 'conscious and conscience'. He will walk to and fro behind the chairs, touching lightly first on one shoulder and then another and, at the same time, keeping up the continuation of his lecture including, with the perfection from long practice, the hesitant contributions from these guests who have joined him on the platform.

He, returning now, comes unexpectedly to a small clearing in the unfamiliar woodland. An unremembered place holding in its strangeness the unwelcome feeling that he is lost and must hurry to find the way back. Overhead is a patch of clear blue sky. A sighing wind emphasises the loneliness of the place. He looks about and discovers that he is not sure from which direction he came into the clearing. He begins, in his own insignificance, to recognise that all the things in his life, which he thinks he loves and respects, are not of any real importance to him. He sets off, with this thought, to find the way where the undergrowth seems to offer something resembling a path.

It seems profitable, while trying to make his way through tough stalks and sharp leaves, to think about Hazel. She is a kind woman. He is grateful to her for the ways in which she 'packs him orf' (her phrase) to concerts and theatres, to his teaching and to conferences. The sounds of her life, the sewing machine, the blender, the dishwasher and the electrolux are all a welcome and a farewell. Hazel and her twin, Chloë, present all too often a back view of their unattractive hips. Both emerge, straightening up from a tangle of weeds, eyes gleaming behind identical spectacles and hair spiked and frizzed by unnoticed twigs and thorns.

Carrying sponge kneelers they have the capacity for being completely absorbed in their planting and weeding. The twin smile of greeting is also one of dismissal.

The Professor, during the discomfort of his walk, wonders why he married one sister and not the other. Pausing in the thicket he feels he has married them both. He does not want to remain where he is and, at the same time, has no real wish to go home. He longs suddenly for snow-covered mountains and cities with onion spires and well-washed trams.

Instead of travelling on the midnight flight, the three of them, Dr Florence, Ms Bianca and the Professor, are staying on at the hotel after the champagne and the final session, the dinner dance.

The Professor, trying to get back in time for his lecture, remembers that Dr Florence, in her innocence, wears her gold-capped fountain pen like a jewel. She has no other ornament. He remembers his responsibility and crashes on through the savage undergrowth:

*Elizabeth Jolley*

*Fair Chloris in a pigsty lay;*
*Her tender herd lay by her . . .*

*Now piercéd is her virgin zone;*
*She feels the foe within it.*

*She hears a broken amorous groan,*
*The panting lover's fainting moan,*
*Just in the happy minute.*

The Professor, out of breath, recalls the lines all too well. Irreverent verse, but with great truth:

*Women can with pleasure feign;*
*Men dissemble still with pain.*

He is dishevelled, torn and dirty, *and* late for his lecture. 'Get real!' he tells himself in self-conscious student speech. The verses, he knows, should have been recited during Hazel's rock cakes and china tea that afternoon. Dr Florence, appreciating the obscure literary approach, catching his glance and unravelling the meaning would have come, ultimately, to an understanding.

He recalls the celebration contained in Traherne's 'Salutation' and his own joy over the three little baby-girl heads neatly asleep on a flat pink sheet. He recalls even more their waking hours. There was never a time without a baby crying. He remembers scrappy lonely meals in dirty airless rooms. He remembers, with distaste, the noise and the smells. There were stained cloths and towels left in the bathroom together with horrible little bowls of liquid with used cotton wool floating in them. He remembers sore stitches, swollen painful breasts and postnatal tears.

He can imagine easily both Dr Florence and Ms Bianca unwashed, unbrushed and unslept, exhausted and quarrelsome, their gowns bloodstained and sour with milk. He can imagine them sobbing, blaming him, saying they have no intention of spending their lives studying the contents of babies' nappies. There is the awful thought that the two pregnancies might result in six babies and they might be boys. How could these two women rear boys? He tries to stop his thoughts . . . When the babies are suddenly thirteen years old with enormous feet and spots . . .

In his room on the twenty-ninth floor of the hotel the Professor is packing his case in a wild and muddled way. When the telephone rings he recognises Hazel's voice at once. In quick small words he asks her to telephone Dr Florence and Ms Bianca.

'Explain I have a headache,' he says. Hazel says yes, she'll do that. She tells him that she has a message for him from Dr Florence and Ms Bianca. Apparently it is the wrong time of the month for them. Hazel says she has confirmed a booking for him on the midnight flight. She reminds him to telephone for a taxi. In the ensuing silence Hazel tells him not to worry about the baby gowns. The machining's done, she says, and she has almost finished the ornamental herringbone stitching at the little necks and the wrists. She will, she says, send the gowns to the Salvation Army. And then she hangs up.

The Professor, reflecting, straight away understands that he has made a mistake. Earlier he had wished for the longed for moments of taking Dr Florence to bed without lies and without secrecy, for hadn't Hazel, apparently completely devoid of jealousy, encouraged the plan? At that time he was aching to hold Dr Florence in his arms, the only flaw being Ms Bianca who was, no doubt, expecting fair play, as arranged, *her turn*.

Because of his wishes and his thoughts he has to understand that he really does have a headache. The pain reassures him, his own honesty being unquestionable in the circumstances.

'Are you a lesbian?' A final question comes from the back of the auditorium.

'No, actually I'm a widow,' the visiting poet's reply is greeted by a round of applause in which approval and amusement are clearly shown. The Professor thanks the visitor for her illuminating lecture and then he and Dr Florence take the visitor to the staff club for a whisky before escorting her to her car.

Later, sitting in his own car, he is grateful that his battery is flat when he is conveniently in front of the fish and chip shop where he stopped to collect a dinner to take home. Burrowing into the parcel he eats a few chips. He watches the crescent moon, with her attendant planet, sinking inexplicably towards a ragged horizon of familiar suburban trees and rooftops. Dr Florence and Ms Bianca will, like the moon and the faithful Venus, be sinking comfortably into an evening of intimacy in their shared apartment. His knowledge of the moon being purely poetical he has no understanding of this early descent. It seems to him that both the moon and Dr Florence are able to enjoy enviable arrangements though he has, for some time, had reservations, never admitted, about Ms Bianca and her interpretation of fidelity. He suspects that she is, beneath her outward show of suggestive adoration, capable of faithlessness. It is possible too that even her infidelity could be only an enactment. He is certain that Dr Florence is unaware of his disturbing suspicions and it would not be proper for him to try to enlighten her. He has been on campus long enough to know something of the treachery of academic revenge; some-times over the slightest thing, the privileged places depending on seniority, for example in the depart-mental car parks. He recalls easily one such breakdown in authority over the ridiculous exposure of the Valen-tine cards being exchanged between Sugarbaby and Cupcake, two ageing and respectable lecturers in anatomy, and physiology, two men old-fashioned enough to have the occasional corpse on display instead of the more attractive models of the human body, now available for demonstration, in washable coloured plastic. The story was on all the front pages, not just the tabloids, with pathetic photographs, chopped reporting and misquotation. And what had this achieved, apart from a show of vindictive jealousy from an unimportant junior member of staff, and the memorable statement from the physiologist's wife: 'I'll not divorce him, not when he's at retirement and his lump sum's due.'

He will not be alone himself this evening. Hazel and Chloë will have returned during the afternoon untidily tanned, windswept and unwashed from a bird-watching expedition. They will have, matching their enthusiasm, hair wild with leaves, bits of dried grass and twigs. They will have endured uncomfortable and, in his opinion, unreasonable demands. One of these being a night-duty watch while perched in a homemade tree house. Hazel, lowering her voice with reverence, says the precarious erection is called a 'hide'. From this sacred place they will have observed the very private nocturnal habits of a certain bird. All this being the reason for the bought dinner, there being no one at home to do the cooking. With his long fingers the professor draws out a few more chips. He is tired and hungry and the unexpected delay is unwelcome.

The woman from the fish shop has knocked twice on his car window to tell him that the jump leads are on their way, but what with the traffic at this time of the evening . . . God himself knows and he won't split . . .

Reflecting on the audacious question (the Professor had not been able to place the voice) and the poet's simple reply, he has to admit that in spite of his admiration and ability to appreciate the poetry of Wilmot, Earl of Rochester, and Chaucer, and their vivid, explicit language – especially Chaucer when spoken in the melodious Middle English, he is mostly unable to adjust to the simulated boldness which accompanies the unnecessary use of vulgar expressions brought in, perhaps self-consciously, to contemporary poetry. The Professor prefers Wilmot's sweet mound of womanly invitation, his 'soft anvil' rather than the unimaginative ugliness of 'cunt'. This word was, he noted, uttered several times by the lady poet during her lecture.

Chloë, spoken in Greek, this name means 'a green shoot'. Chloë, a delicate green shoot. The name is sometimes given to the Goddess of the harvest (fruit in particular), Demeter or Ceres, she is known by both names. The Professor, imagining for a moment, the delicate love between Daphnis and the shepherdess, Chloë, feels that the name is both romantic and poetical and not really suitable for Hazel's sister, but then who could know how sweet and refined this sister's thoughts might be. She has shown herself, at times, to be capable of moving her large body with an unexpected grace. One particular time, he recalls, was round the kitchen table, vegetable knife in hand, taking dainty little steps in perfect time with the charming and famous Boccherini minuet; part of a Sunday personal choice radio program, full on, in competition with Hazel's blender and other appliances.

The image of the hefty Chloë has persisted. In particular when the Professor, preparing to go to bed and anticipating the pleasure of placing his pen, his watch and chain, along with the small change from his pockets, on the bedside table, this idea, this image of Chloë dancing, the memory of this single occasion, returns to him time and again, suggesting the possibility of bringing his own noble and perhaps strange thoughts to enrich the rather more limited world of this other person, his sister-in-law, Chloë.

During the repeated moment of this small and humble action, that of removing his pen, his watch, the gold chain and the small change from his person, he understands, with a shock, that he wishes to be admired. Especially he wishes to be admired and awaited. The removal and careful placing of these masculine items is a symbol of his being available for the act of chivalry. He is in the process of undressing.

On the day of the legendary minuet (Chloë's eloquent skirts a mixture of display and concealment), there was a tender light filtering through the green foliage outside the kitchen window. The linoleum, designed to look like old tiles, caressed by Hazel's bare feet for many years, seemed dark and luxurious. Blue and white china caught the soft light and became translucent.

The light, the music and Chloë's dance went unnoticed by Hazel. She, on that occasion, did not notice her husband's ardent hem-kissing presence either. He is accustomed, in a restful way, to being unnoticed. And it is the same in the department. He moves along the corridors, exchanging fond and conventional greetings absent-mindedly. He knows that Dr Florence and Ms Bianca meet on deeper levels. For them he does not represent another wished-for world. Their entire existence, in each other, is all too complete and familiar, though he knows that Dr Florence, with a quiet wisdom, always keeps back something of herself. If and when Ms Bianca pouts and flounces, Dr Florence is capable of a shrug. She has pretty shoulders, pretty *and* magnificent.

That Chloë's dance should be unnoticed by her twin is natural in that Hazel, unable as a small child to pronounce 'Chloë', named her sister 'Clover', a name which later had to be formally dismissed in favour of the more classical and beautiful 'Chloë', her given name.

Mother, his mother, he always thinks of her as Mother. Mother taught him to dance. When he was quite young, his mother and his twin sister (of whom he was very fond), took him round the floor, first one and then the other, teaching him the steps, the turnings, left and right, back and forth and, at the same time, showing him the correct way to hold his partner's hand and, more importantly, where to place his other hand, lightly, yet with authority. And perhaps even more, the most important of all, they demonstrated the ways in which he had, simultaneously, to yield and command, the twin movements in time and in step with the music. He began, at once then, to love dancing.

During the dancing he discovered that the supposedly intimate moments of touching were in innocence because of the requirements of the dance itself. Certain steps and figures, which were in themselves the expression and the meaning of the dance and its wider representative qualities, could cause the partners to be deeply aware of each other yet still able to regard the often unexpected excitement and apparent response as being simply a part of the dance.

The little bow and the curtsey were the ordinary conventional invitation, the ordinary well-mannered behaviour, together with the subdued gentle applause at the end of the dance.

It was at a dance, he recalls easily, that he first met Hazel and Chloë. They, in turn, had become reliable partners, first one and then the other. He often smiles remembering his confusion. It was difficult to tell them apart. It was during the time, in his reading, when he was deeply immersed in the *Chloris* poems. He seemed then to be seeing people and events as if through the eyes of the one-time Earl of Rochester, and, for fun, he named both young women 'Chloris', but privately. And then, more boldly, he called them by this name. Having the same name for both girls, he discovered, disposed of the worry of getting them mixed up and giving each the other's name. They, not knowing the poem, but liking the name and his gentle brown eyes, answered to both the name and the eyes.

He never revealed to them the connection with the pigsty. He often consoled himself during the more clumsily managed household arrangements and tasks by reciting poetry to himself in a soft whisper. During the more startling aspects of family life with the very small but very intrusive babies, the triplets, a little relevant quotation, he often had the thought, might bring the welcome relief of relaxation and laughter. But he was never, during that time, courageous enough to recite to his audience of two:

> *Fair Chloris in a pigstye lay*
> *Her tender herd lay by her*

In any case he would have to leave out the moans accompanying an approaching climax.

> *Rescue your bosom pig from fate*
> *Who now expires, hung in the gate*
> *That leads to Flora's cave.*

Hazel and Chloë, they are ugly sisters without

any of the well-known qualities belonging to the original ugly sisters. For one thing they are both hard-working and would never think of piling menial work upon anyone. They are jovial in an almost mannish way. They are not in the least selfish or vain. He suspects that they never look in any mirror, not even the oval one in the hall which invites a last minute's anxious glance from anyone leaving the house. They both give the impression of not knowing what they are wearing, as if they had hurriedly pulled on some garments earlier in the morning. They are never unkind in thought or speech but express opinions in brief, fair-minded words. Honesty being the most important issue rather than the kind lie. Both are incapable of jealousy and mean gossip. It is as if there is no room in either of them for the less desirable but, at the same time, protective human aspects of the personality. After all, it is thought that certain attributes – jealousy, for example, revenge, ambition also, and greed and remorse (especially remorse), and even the ability to enjoy rumour and careless unkind words – do provide, not altogether in a negative way, a certain resilience to adversity. In spite of not possessing these particular gifts, there are qualities in both Hazel and Chloë which remind the Professor of the way in which a family-size carton of ice-cream does not melt immediately when put into a car while shopping on a very hot day . . .

The Professor, burdened with fatherhood, thinks of his three daughters (a multiple birth, the memory has never faded) backpacking through Europe and Asia. They have sent messages about the celebration (multiple) which is 'imperative', their word, immediately on their return. Various messages describe this celebration in turn as being a 'rave', a 'rage', a 'gig' and other meaningless words. Coloured flashing lights and a particular band with a name, Computer Shut Down, equally meaningless, have been included in later messages. There has been no mention whatever of the names of the lucky bridegrooms and their families.

These girls, his daughters, with their sweet greedy lips and penetrating voices immediately had their own way with their father. Looking back, it is as if they had leapt from the protection of his lap, his loving hands and knees, to 'Anger', 'Ice' and 'Lust' (lipsticks) to the mood-provoking perfumes, 'Get Real', 'Reckless' and 'Circular', and on to stark white face-powder, pierced ears, nose rings and exotic nipple brooches. They were, they said, making a statement. At the dinner table, after discussing the merits of deodorants and tampons advertised on television, they introduced other topics. They demonstrated their lateral thinking with opinions on marriage, on divorce, on abortion, on orgasm and on counselling. They included in their list shoplifting, drugs, single mother-hood, the homeless, sexual abuse and incest. The Professor, never as a rule at a loss for words, at these times simply looked on, amazed.

The woman from the fish shop is knocking on his window. Something about the jump leads having got hisself a flat and isn't it just like the thing, but, ten, she holds up ten fingers, minutes sure he'll be right here . . . and not to worry . . .

The hairdresser, earlier, said that he knows when the Professor is thinking that too much is being cut off. It seems as if the visit to the hairdresser was a week ago and not just first thing this morning. The hairdresser said he could feel the Prof's anxiety in the tips of his scissors. He went on to assure the Professor that he was just doing a trim as requested, nothing more. He'd see for himself in a little while that it was all hokay and meanwhile he should think his own thoughts and relax. 'Just you relax,' the hairdresser told him.

The Professor, relaxing, wondered if Beethoven was particular about his hair and how it was cut. He then remembered reading about Beethoven, that he wrote the Kreutzer Sonata in 1803 for a violinist, a mulatto, a British subject apparently, called George Augustus Something, Bridge or Tower or both, and that Beethoven deliberately set out to write a piano and violin sonata which had enough dash and bounce in it to suit the violinist. They performed it once together, and later they quarrelled and Beethoven took his sonata home and dedicated it to Kreutzer, who was well known, a French composer and violinist at the

Paris conservatoire. Kreutzer did not appreciate the sonata, did not understand it and never played it.

The Professor would have liked to speak about this but he remembered he was supposed to be relaxing. He fell easily into another thought, that of having seen Chloë's response to the minuet. He was hungry, a strange word but it was a kind of hunger to know the effects on her of, for example, the last part of Mahler's work, *Das Lied von der Erde*, the voluptuous *Abschied*. This music and the rich, thoughtful voice of the contralto lifting – as if floating over mountains and through clouds, sometimes storm clouds or clouds rosy with the innocence of the dawn – would envelop them all. He would like, one day in the kitchen, to take them all by surprise with this music. He reflects now on the differences between people, even between sisters where there are clear similarities.

Hazel and Chloë are a little different from their rather mannish friends, the bird-watching associates. These people, the bird watchers, say 'Crikey' instead of the 'Golly-Gosh' which Hazel and Chloë brought with them, a legacy from their English boarding school, together with another useful gift, the ability to dress and undress inside their top clothes or inside a towel, wrapped around, without being in the least mysterious, provocative or indecent.

But then the mysterious was being removed from life every day. He almost spoke of this to the hairdresser who is much more than a simple barber, being a *coiffeur*, a Specialist in Hair. He is a man with strong original views on almost any subjects which come to mind while his customer is in the special chair. The Professor, wisely, did not speak then, knowing that any conversation is destined to become animated and the Designer of Hair will, in his enthusiasm over the discussion, simply abandon himself to the art of cutting, chopping even, of what little hair remains . . .

On the previous visit this had happened during a fantastic exchange of memories about drains, leaving the Professor almost bald with what could only be considered a sort of prison or hospital hair cut. He remembers still the cold air on his skull as he left the studio. He actually wished then that he had, of all things, a head scarf. Nothing cheap, of course, and nothing fancy. A square, his thoughts had become elaborate, a square would be best, folded into a triangle, a fine cashmere with a paisley design in bluish-grey colours, nothing noisy or vulgar . . .

It was true though, the mysterious in everyday life was disappearing. He remembers, frequently, the one-time sweet eagerness of his daughters when they were little girls. They embraced, with excitement and joy, every new or repeated experience. He recalls their homecoming one Easter, twelve-year-old schoolgirls, coming home for the Easter break, excited over chocolate rabbits and Easter eggs hidden in the garden . . .

At the end of the very next term, they explained that during the last week they had been given something called Sex Education. Every girl had received, handed out in class, a neat little personal kit in readiness for the onset of menstruation. Included in every kit were two condoms with instructions for their use. The girls had practised rolling them on and off each other's fingers, the whole class and their teacher Mr Norton (Assist. Maths and Physics) taking part.

They had posters too, they said, to pin up in their bedrooms. They couldn't wait, they said, to pin them up. Hazel pointed out, while she served a baked custard, that the symptoms for anything looked worse on the printed page. She said, also, that the one thing the girls should have been told, with all this free information, was that they should know a person's name before getting into bed with him or her. If possible, she added, their mothers should know each other.

Hazel was full of surprises. The Professor has, over the years, had to admit this to himself. Seeing the symptoms and the stages of venereal infections, in black and white (headings in caps), on the walls of his daughters' bedrooms was ominous and the accompanying illustrations were hideous, completely lacking in poetry or beauty. He wondered, while his scalp was being massaged with professional determination, why the male organ is always depicted hanging in such a dejected and defeated way. As the only male in a houseful of women and girls, he feels degraded by the diagram of the male. Though fully clothed, he feels ashamed of his own body lurking in the bleak company

97

of the posters. In addition he has suffered a considerable shock over the drawing of 'The Female Organs of Generation'.

To begin with he simply did not recognise them. With his own romantic imagery persisting, he was unable to place the parts in relation to the whole female body, 'feminine', he prefers this word rather than female, the whole *feminine* body. Where, for example, was that all important and inviting entrance? He gazed at the insistent title, uncomprehending.

'It's a section, Father,' one of the girls explained.

'Yes, Father, it's easy, it's simply as if the female has been sliced,' the Middle Triplet told him.

'Sliced up,' the Third and Smallest Triplet said. 'Sliced right up through here,' she said, demonstrating with the complicated gymnastics of a contortionist involving her whole body, her arms and hands and her legs. 'A vertical slice, Father, right up through here,' she told him.

'Ah! Yes, I see,' the Father said then, knowing that, as Father or even as Professor, he did not see. But all this was some time ago . . .

'That will be thirty dollars exactly.' The Designer of Hair had a way of bringing his clients out of their 'relaxations'. He was able to hold his heavy mirror forcing the Professor to see the nape of his own neck, vulnerable as always after an appointment, once again without the soft brown curls which were scattered across the linoleum.

His daughters would be returning home shortly the Professor told the hairdresser as he was leaving, and the hairdresser said he would be pleased to attend to their needs, that is, if the young ladies had given away their shaved heads.

The Professor, the Father, jolted by this remark, had to remind himself, all over again, that these returning daughters were no longer the long-haired, long-legged, laughing schoolgirls who came, always larger than the time before, bursting into the quiet household for the school holidays, but are now well-travelled young women with startling, mind-shaking (their expression) ideas, and with all kinds of knowledge and opinions and, of course, the bald heads or perhaps, hopefully, they will be stubbled heads.

Now he anxiously contemplates the immediate future, the multiple celebration, the multiple marriage – three weddings simultaneously. He prefers to remember the girls, home from boarding school, moving with grace between the substantial armchairs, offering dinner guests black coffee and Turkish delight. In particular he likes to remember the cosy and intimate times after dinner, when all the guests had left, and the girls, laughing together, brushed each other's long hair in front of the remains of the sitting-room fire. The embers, glowing still, made their cheeks red and sent golden-brown lights through their hair. That was before they had their heads shaved.

For the forthcoming wedding, the Professor, not having the imagination to envisage the celebration, makes a great effort to recall all the wedding celebrations he has endured during the years. He tries to think . . .

'Think, Daddy! Think Positive!' the girls always reminded him at the appropriate times, Christmas and, of course, the Birthday. He remembers an archway of devoted wedding guests on one occasion.

Certainly it was striking. A guard of honour, that was it. The girls should have a guard of honour. He has no military background himself and, when he considers this, neither have any of their friends or immediate colleagues. Not a sword or a gun, not a weapon between them.

The whole wedding, from the beginning, has presented itself as if set in a medieval scene or perhaps something during the Renaissance or even in a Shakespearean play. In this way this removes his effort of thought, without intention, from the present which is, he understands, quite beyond him, to a more possible time in the past. The idea of a medieval pageant is appealing . . .

Suddenly he has an idea, a guard of honour could be created with flowers. He extracts and chews on a piece of fish. He is probably, against his principles, eating shark or something protected like a dolphin. With fish and chip shops you could never know . . .

He thinks once more of flowers, long-stemmed irises held aloft and arching. Blue, yellow and white irises, graceful flowers, the colours of Easter. An Easter wedding. Blue for the bridesmaids' dresses, the pages should be dressed in yellow and the brides, of course, would wear white. The brides should have embroidered, on their dresses, breastplates of pure white lace in the elaborate patterns of either the Mechlin or the Honiton.

Three brides' dresses and six dresses for bridesmaids, two bridesmaids for each bride and, of course, six little pages for the same reason. It was possible that the families of the bridegrooms might bear the financial responsibility, for example, of dressing the bridesmaids and the pages and even supplying the flowers and the bartenders' wages. His mind racing, he wonders about the variations in cost of the different kinds of champagne. He anticipates sleepless nights. He supposes, unwillingly, that the bridegrooms and their families will need suitable accommodation since they must be from somewhere in Europe. Depending on their backgrounds there could be possible differences in the kind of accommodation offered. He has no way of knowing whether these people are educated and cultured or merely hard-working peasants. He supposes the wedding, which will be a big affair, will be required very soon after the homecoming. Perhaps immediately. Young people, his daughters especially, have never wanted to wait for anything. He admits he would like them to wait for certain *instruction*. He has in mind 'The Rules of Courtly Love'. He can recite many of the wise sayings from Andreas Capellanus (twelfth century), not all of them are applicable at this stage, but surprisingly many speak the truth he wants to offer:

*Love is a certain inborn suffering derived from the sight of an excessive meditation upon the beauty of the opposite sex, which causes each one to wish above all things the embraces of the other and by common desire to carry out all of love's precepts in the other's embrace.*

And then the rules:

1 *Marriage is no real excuse for not loving.*
2 *He who is not jealous cannot love.*
3 *No one can be bound by a double love.*

Losing the concentration of memory, the Professor imagines a church wedding. He even visualises a fine day with a warm light breeze and a blessing of gentle sunshine. He will continue the recitation of the rules at the moment when they will be needed . . .

Meanwhile there will have to be arrangements with the local hotel (as well as the church), the ballroom at the hotel will be needed *and* the charming and business-like manageress – and her staff will need to be engaged . . . He remembers a colleague, a father of twins, having a special jacket made for his daughters' double wedding. The jacket, a perfect fit, was of blue silk with a deeper blue taffeta lining. It rustled pleasantly. He supposes he will need new clothes and so will Hazel. He hesitates, Hazel is quite capable of being at the wedding in an old calico smock complete with a straw hat and gardening shoes . . . He fumbles for a handkerchief, his fingers are all over grease.

Appropriate music will be needed. He likes the bridal-chamber scene with the Wedding March at the opening of Act III in Wagner's *Lohengrin*. And perhaps, even better, there is Bach's *Wedding Cantata* in which the soprano, blessing the newly wedded, sings of a world reborn, completely renewed and inspiring eternal love and happiness . . .

Thinking of clothes, going back to clothes, he can imagine that other women, knowing they were shabby and unfashionable, would arrive badly dressed and cringing. But Hazel, her mind on other things, remains forever beyond the reaches of shallow fashion. The daughters have ways of dealing with this. They manage with phrases: 'Oh! you *know* Mother!' and, with little high-pitched squeals of laughter and shrugging of shoulders, would say once more: 'Oh, *you know Mother!*' and 'Just look at Mother's hat, it's positively disintegrating. Mother, *Darling!* your *hat!*'

With her splendid cutting-out scissors and her ability to follow a pattern accurately, Hazel will no doubt be very successful with his new jacket, but not blue silk, that is not *him*. He will think of the jacket and its colour later.

*'Tis not an easy thing to be entirely happy but to be kind is very easy* . . . The words have come into his mind. He receives them with pleasure. Of course he

will be expected to prepare a speech. The wise and perhaps even reassuring quotation from Wilmot, Earl of Rochester, taken from a letter he wrote to his wife in 1669, would offer an excellent theme for the whole tone of the wedding. He tries to speak the words aloud, rolling them in his mouth, recalling them from memory. The Earl of Rochester, loose, disorderly and immoral, rises above his life of debauchery when he addresses his wife:

*'Tis not an easy thing to be entirely happy, but to be kind is very easy, and that is the greatest measure of happiness. I say not this to put you in mind of being kind to me; you have practised that so long that I have a joyful confidence you will never forget it; but to show that I myself have a sense of what the methods of my life seem so utterly to contradict.*

Perhaps, after his eloquence, all three bridegrooms, in the first person, might be moved towards a declaration, a protestation of purity as a symbolic act of contrition, to offer to the brides, in advance, to accompany them throughout their lives.

What husbands are lying in wait for his daughters? Are the future husbands related to each other, a father and two sons with an eye to building, from the strength of a multiple marriage, a successful business? A woman with three oafish louts for sons and a houseful of unclaimed brats to bring with them? Or simply three men neither wise nor handsome and certainly not rich but old and needing someone to cook and clean for them? His thoughts are depressing.

Fortunately the arrival of the jump leads creates a diversion. New life enters the battery.

At home the Professor speaks of the uneasiness of there being no names for the bridegrooms.

'Names? Bridegrooms? Wedding?' Hazel is throwing away the greasy remains of the parcel she has gathered from the front seat of the car.

'Bridegrooms?' She pauses, reaching for a frozen quiche. 'Wedding? It's not a wedding,' she says quite kindly for someone who has *waited and* been deprived of the evening meal. 'It's all right,' she says as she sees the Professor's uneasy recognition of the quiche; one of Hazel's vegetarian creations resembling something which can be found in grassy fields where herds grazing lavishly replenish and enrich the earth at frequent intervals.

'It's spinach,' Hazel says, 'Chloë and I . . .'

'Yes, yes of course,' the Professor says quickly. 'I seem to have eaten already.'

'It's not a wedding,' Hazel says again with patience. 'It's their birthday, the girls,' she says, 'it's their twenty-first birthday party. Remember? The girls will be twenty-one.' She puts the dish in the oven and turns the heat to high.


The Professor, later in his study, listens to the Mozart quartet *The Hunt*. He is resting with a glass of pinot noir on the small table at his side. The whole load of a wedding is lifted, by Hazel's simple explanation, from his mind. A party that is all, a simple birthday party. (He has always enjoyed blowing up the balloons.) The twenty-first celebration can be approached with light footsteps and an even lighter heart.

He enjoys, very much, the quartet. He likes the idea of the musicians keeping time and pace by regarding each other, from time to time, with unmistakeable tenderness; sometimes even with deference, and actually, in their playing, seeming to be in perfect compliance one with another. He envies this communication between the musicians. They question and reply without words. There is the moment of pause, and then with touching gratitude in expression and a slight bowing of the head, an expected acknowledgement allows the resumption of exact and timely accompaniment. Listening, he feels as if he is watching the performance.

The music in *The Hunt* leaps forward in a spirited gallop and then quickly becomes more thoughtful and more complicated. The Professor has discovered, over the years, that it is not possible to sing, with the human voice, the opening sounds of *The Hunt*.

During the evening he comes to the conclusion that seeing the crescent moon descending, accompanied by Venus, was rather like eating fish and chips straight out of the wrapping paper. Both experiences should be shared with someone. Alone, they were nothing.

*I*t occurs to the Professor quite suddenly that during the whole time of the staff meeting his thoughts have wandered. He has been inhabiting a castle, a small one surrounded by a moat and set in peaceful green meadows some time in the late fourteenth century. And, during this time, this imagined experience, Hazel and Chloë, benign and portly, have been walking together in the near distance of these grass-covered fields, suitably clothed, as usual, as if for gardening or bird watching in the modern suburb. Making a concession to the change of century, both are wearing the wimple. The Professor imagines each wimple being made from the purest white linen and freshly laundered. In consideration of some of the more tiresome difficulties of the times (the late CXIV) Hazel and Chloë, in hushed voices, could be discussing methods for catching fleas. Straining his hearing, the Professor is managing to hear their voices. Both are speaking in low and serious tones. Hazel seems to be saying: *Item, dear sister, blanchets of white wool set on straw, and on the bed, and when black fleas should hop on them they are sooner found upon the white sheet and killed . . . when coverlets, furs or dresses wherein there be fleas, be folded and shut tightly up, as in a chest tightly corded with straps, or in a bag . . .* Chloë, excited, joins in, *well tied up and pressed, so that the aforesaid fleas be without light and air and kept imprisoned, then they will perish forthwith and die . . .*

The Professor, letting the imagined castle and the voices drift, supposes that he is retreating (not necessarily from the staff meeting which is progressing well without any attention or input – staff word – from him), but from the inevitable celebrations, multiple, which are immediately ahead. Even more on his mind is the recent early morning – one a.m. – arrival at the international airport of his three daughters and an unexpected guest. One man, as it were, shared with an admirable if disturbing possessiveness, equally by the triplets.

At present, during the monotonous but well-bred discussion at the table, he has to understand that it is hard to know what to make of this guest, hidden as he is, surgically, and made more mysterious by his first request on arrival at the house. They were still in the hall when he asked, demanded really, a mozzarella sandwich, *without the vinaigrette*, so that he could, as he said *feel* the mozzarella, the *flavour*, on his tongue. As well as the mozzarella in his nylon backpack, suspended carelessly across the handles of his wheelchair, he had also a jar of chocolate cream from Italy, flown with him from Italy, chocolate and finely ground nuts, nut chocolate to be melted in a small saucepan and allowed to drip slowly over soft white bread.

It was Hazel who made the suggestion that the chocolate dripping could wait and that bed was the best place for them all, as soon as a bed was made up for the guest. It was Hazel and Chloë, with muscled arms, who reached into the linen cupboard for sheets and blankets. And it was Chloë who picked up, in the porch, the battered teddy bear which apparently inhabited the stranger's luggage. It was Chloë also who pulled out the sofa bed.

All three daughters, the Professor is even more disturbed to recall, wanted to put the young man to bed. That he required nursing was clear at once. He had to be helped, at the airport, from his wheelchair into the car and then later from the car to the wheelchair.

The unexpected guest seems to have many broken bones, or destroyed body tissue, from the number of splints, plaster casts and bandages. His condition, the Professor thinks, must be serious. And, from the shrill squabbling between his daughters about taking turns to look after the guest, it is clear that the household is about to be severely disrupted.

The Professor, as the meeting progresses slowly through its hour, wearily imagines the lack of peace and the tiresome presence, inevitably, of nurses. The physical and emotional nursing of a young man so severely handicapped by the damage he has suffered is surely intimate and therefore needing a professional approach.

Nurses. The Professor has a great respect for them and their knowledge of the mysterious. This sense of their intimate knowledge would have encouraged, at one time, the Professor to marry a nurse, but since one did not appear on his horizon he proposed to Hazel and, with all honesty, has no real regrets. He must make his daughters, straight away, understand the need for a nurse – two, to allow for suitable shifts.

Nurses. He often thought that if his baby daughters, when they were newly born, had had bigger ears, the nurse could and would have carried them bunched all three, at once, by their ears as rabbits were often picked up and carried. He had imagined the babies then, and recalls this easily now, as being quite silent when carried in this way and, in the face of this, being capable of great endurance and imperceptively grateful, finally, to be allowed to burrow their little round heads once more into the harsh sheets of their little cots, these utilitarian, almost prison-like, regulation hospital cribs. The Professor, the Father, completely absorbed in this vivid recollection of something purely imaginative, smiles into the lapels of his jacket as he stands at the door to shake hands with the members of staff as they leave the meeting. On his way to his own room he continues to smile, giving himself up to the thoughts of the sweet eagerness of his little girls, especially as they were when advancing from rapid crawling to being upright for one or two hesitant steps before sitting down backwards and having to struggle up all over again.

Still smiling and perhaps losing the smile, he sits down at his desk. One of the benefits of being Professor and Father is that, in the department and at home, cups of tea are brought to him at specific times. He sips his tea and reflects quietly that at airports the travellers are all reduced to a kind of ugliness.

Something of this ugliness has come home, half hidden, with his daughters. Being occupied with themselves and their demanding guest, they have not been eager to describe their adventures. Mostly, the Professor thinks, people who have travelled want an audience. Often they talk too much in rather a conceited way and they always have far too many photographs. The daughters have not, it seems, been impressed by a painting, a building (not even a church), a bridge or a mountain.

There was the time, he remembers with pleasure, when he visited the *Jungfraujoch*, the highest mountain among the Swiss Alps. The journey took five trains and six hours. In spite of three fainting fits (the air being so rare), he was able to appreciate the cloud formations and the impressive scenery at intervals in the parting and the drifting of the clouds.

And then there was the unforgettable moment when he was actually standing on the pavement, in Vienna, in front of the entrance of the famous *Krankenhaus* where Schubert, making reluctant unavoidable visits, would have hesitated for as long as possible, frightened of the inevitable final incarceration, before being dragged across the threshold of that place which was no better than an infected madhouse.

Standing there, then, he had tried to recall the little dances and the delicate tenderness captured in the music which Schubert was writing. He remembers also that he vomited.

He must clear his untidy desk. He will find an examiner for the inadequate thesis which has gathered dust for several months and he will tell the young writer of a lengthy first novel that she has talent.

And, while dealing with all this, he thinks, with a small careworn smile, of the very young, young woman who has what is called 'a crush' on him. He is unable to understand her poems but is deeply moved that she has written them. Her thin, cold hands have a starved roughness about them, as if she has to do a great deal of scrubbing for very little food. He notices this every time when, accidentally, his hands brush against hers while they are passing pages to and fro. He can see that all three students have special qualities and are in love with their phrases, but all need direc- tion and discipline (especially Ms Novelist). A moment of desperation inspires him to suggest that all three have a discussion, in general terms, over lunch with him one day (the staff club rather than his presently overcrowded house). In this way the three of them can talk with animation to each other thus leaving him to his own thoughts.

He lifts the telephone to ask his secretary. 'June?' he says. Marie reminds him that June left six months and more ago, but what can she, Marie, do for him.

Lunch? Sure, she will phone the three young women and the staff club. And, with the promise of a reminder call on the day, it is all arranged.

*Every aspect of human energy is exciting.*

Henry James

$D$r Florence, unable to come to terms (departmental phrase), with the process of insemination and the resulting inconvenience of pregnancy, to say nothing of the pain and the rather messy things of childbirth, has decided on adoption and that is why they, Dr Florence, Ms Bianca and the Professor are in the waiting room at the orphanage. The appointment was put off earlier because Dr Florence was indisposed. The Professor understands perfectly, women vary. Hazel and Chloë, over the years, were usually in tandem with their monthly migraine. (The 'migraine' was their little joke since they did not suffer from headaches.) They never excused themselves, they were never indisposed. It was easy to imagine them both, as teenagers, brandishing their hockey sticks, never missing a single match (destined to play for Britain), ignoring Matron's pacifying little pink notes of explanation to their gym mistress, requesting a few days free from physical education and sport.

The Professor has accompanied the two women as Hazel, whose idea it was to adopt – possibly weekends only because of Dr Florence's teaching load and subsequent marking – has pointed out that his presence, as a sort of surrogate relative to the babies, would give more status to the two women and their claim.

As they sit in the well-polished room the Professor allows his thoughts to wander into his deep regard for Dr Florence and how he would have sustained all in his power to please her in the feeling of relaxation and release created during and after lovemaking as well, of course, as the serious intention to insemi-nate. He does not dwell on the possibility that, as her lover he might, with the present relationship between the two women, be unwanted. He confesses inwardly his disappointment which is, in all honesty, mixed with relief.

He has often noticed that Dr Florence possesses

unusual courage. She sometimes parks her car on the edge of a nightmarish main road . . . surrounded by uninhabited waste land, an industrial area of unrepaired factories used for the processing of pet food . . . in order to visit a special nursery and rose garden flourishing there unexpectedly. He is always shocked to remember that offal and unmentionable bits of cow carcases were melted down into a product essential in the making of ice-cream. It is impossible for him to imagine the cold cleanliness, the white purity of a family tub of vanilla ice-cream being polluted in this way.

Somewhere a piano is being played and childish voices are labouring through 'All Things Bright and Beautiful'. The Professor comments on the length of the hymn and that they are to have an even longer wait. The two women do not have anything to say though the Professor notices, with renewed astonishment, that since they have been sharing a study (this in itself is unusual especially as Ms Bianca is not officially on the staff), Dr Florence is adopting the same clichéd body language employed by Ms Bianca. This includes both the friendly gestures and the more hostile movements. Among these there is the dipping of the head, a quick forward movement accompanying certain figures of speech, 'that's your problem' and 'tell that to the marines', the quick sidelong glance and the twisted smile, the withdrawn hands, the firmly folded arms, the shoulders turning inwards and one knee cocked over the other leg so that the whole body is turned away, with a wordless brutality, during a conversation. Alternatively there is the clichéd imitation seductiveness stolen from the pages of the fashion magazines, an irritating, almost successful part of Ms Bianca's repetoire which, so far, Dr Florence has not added to her own. He can only imagine that this new need for body language reflects, in Dr Florence, an inner conflict or unhappiness, and he, without wanting to impose himself too heavily on her, feels that he should perhaps, at some time, gently suggest that sharing a study is not an accepted custom in the department. He is sure the sharing is Ms Bianca's idea, therefore he should really tell her to take her things and leave. Not so simple, he told Hazel late one evening when he had been brooding on the problem.

Hazel thinks that he could speak in a sort of fatherly way to both women. She is of the opinion that they both, in plain words, have been broody for quite some time. She said also, at the time, that Dr Florence falls down badly in the body language and her attempts to imitate and master it. And this in itself, she said, was a good sign.

There are several baby photographs on the waiting-room walls. The Professor, confronted by a fat-faced little individual who has both fists raised and clenched, and a very stern expression, a direct gaze from beneath an authoritarian brow, feels suddenly as if he is looking at his immediate successor. He will remember to tell Hazel and Chloë later, with a little laugh at his own expense. He remembers, too, that he wants to tell Hazel and Chloë about the pigeon and his mating dance. Even though Hazel and Chloë are ardent bird watchers, far more seriously than he is himself (after all he does not even leave his desk to watch the pigeons), it is likely that the description of the male pigeon's devoted and tireless efforts will be wasted on them.

'I've got two of my very special babies ready for adoption,' the matron of the orphanage, her voice rich with an unexpected Orphean excellence, comes singing into the waiting room.

'Please come into my office.' She leads the way across the room, flinging wide her door. 'Weekends,' she says, 'but please sit down, sit down, weekends would suit beautifully, that way their school work won't be interrupted.' Her gracious smile matches her generous voice and figure. The Professor, reflecting, imagines how well she would carry an advertisement for bathroom tiles, wall-to-wall carpets and leather lounges in lavish television commercials.

'School work?' Dr Florence and Ms Bianca lean forward in a simultaneous movement. The Professor hears their voices cracking in horrified unison.

'Yes,' the matron is leafing through a pile of papers, 'we're just coming up to our tenth and eleventh birthday. We don't talk hardly at all, shy and quiet; we just grunt at this age, vocab is fine,' she reassures her small audience. 'It's just a stage we're at . . . You'll agree it's better than those small bundles bawling all day and all night ...' There is a small silence as the door is opened from the other side just enough for two boys, shuffling their feet, to be encouraged by unseen hands into the room.

'These two, as you can see,' the matron smiles through her words, 'they'll be no trouble. Not like girls who never stop talking and always wanting new ribbons and new dresses. These two are very nice boys, twins from a good family.' The matron pauses and then continues, 'The same mother but a different father, a year apart they are, but you'll agree they're real look-a-likes, the spitting image of each other. You'll *adore* them. Freddy, this one nearest me, is the bright one, bright as two buttons and Teddy, the little one, he's got a lovely nature.' Teddy, head down, is trying to hide behind Freddy.

There is a short silence as the boys are gazed upon by Dr Florence and Ms Bianca. Meanwhile the Professor notices a correction to the matron's expected title. His attention is drawn to a neatly printed little tablet, on the wall, immediately behind her, carrying the ornamental words:

## DIRECTOR OF RESIDENTIAL MANAGEMENT

There is, as well, a picture of the orphanage on another wall and, with a sudden quickening of intelligence, he understands that the name 'orphanage' is not used any more. The establishment in the framed photograph is described as St Monica's Residential College. He understands that he needs to keep up with the changing world, with the ordinary facts as they change, and with the new and special language which everyone else seems to know and to use.

'Pardon me for asking,' the director continues, 'is it the three of you as is having the boys? A threesome, is it?'

Dr Florence, having no voice suddenly, looks with imploring eyes at the Professor. Ms Bianca is studying her finger nails.

'Oh, there will be several of us, a whole houseful, very jolly,' the Professor says quickly. 'No, not a commune, a household. Awfully jolly,' he laughs, 'you understand,' trying to be jovial and yet responsible. 'Weekends, house and garden sort of thing.

Wheelbarrow,' he says, 'er, lawn mower, grass, wash the car etc.'

The management, bestowing gracious smiles, says, 'A number of our boys and gels are weekenders. It's a *beautiful* arrangement. Some of our truly beautiful people don't ever want to separate from their partial little adoptions.' She pauses and straightens Freddy's spectacles. 'You're very wise,' she continues, 'to have them a bit bigger. They've grown a bit and are a bit stronger. Don't get so many colds and coughs when they've grown a bit.' She turns to the boys who have not raised their eyes to glance at the guests.

'Run along now, boys, the both of you. There might well be an outing for you, the beach or the zoo this very next weekend . . .' The boys disappear as if the same capable hands which, unseen, brought about their discreet entrance, are assisting them in leaving.

'There are a few teeny things, teensy weensy details,' the director says. 'I'll run them by you and then the ball's in your court. I'll be frank,' she leans forwards as if in confidence, 'the bottom line is simply head lice. I have to ask that some simple combing is done before the boys return. They will be combed before they leave, it's very simple really.'

'Yes, yes, of course,' the Professor wants the director to know that he is familiar with every problem of childhood, though this one is new.

'We supply the toothcombs and the lotion, it's really only what we call a prophylactic measure.'

'Yes, yes, of course.' The Professor is trying to appear at ease with the circumstances which are more than a little sinister; for one thing the phrase, 'the bottom line', contains, surely, something called 'a hidden agenda'.

'The boys will have a clean bill of health every time they leave the "Residential" and we expect a clean ditto ditto when they return.' The director starts to gather her papers.

The Professor is unable to recognise a word of truth in the expression 'a clean bill of health'. For him it is associated with politicians trying to hide something which the public ought to know. A visual image to demonstrate his association could be a clean, neat, figure-of-eight bandage hiding a festering and terrible wound, something incurable and offensive even to the most insensitive nose. Without wanting to, he thinks of the young man, the Victim, the Incubus. What is lurking beneath all those splints and surgical wrapping? Who is the man his daughters have brought home and what does he want? What will he take . . .? And worse, what will he give, leave behind him?

'Remember, the ball's in your court.' The director is smiling at them all in turn. She thumbs through some more of her paperwork, with a little sigh, as if she needs a particular page.

'I would take those two boys myself . . .' she murmurs, 'but just you put on your thinking caps and give us a bell when you're ready to stop by and clinch the deal.'

The Professor's mind, active with disaster, is full of decayed teeth, incredible virus (untreatable) infections, low-grade throat inflammations, athlete's foot and worms and now the head lice. He knows the louse family is an extended family, three varieties of lice, head, body and pubic. *Pediculosis capitas*, *Pediculosis corporis* and *Pediculosis pubis*. He recalls sitting in the back of the lecture hall while Cupcake and Sugar, his highly esteemed colleagues, demonstrated with a delicious quiet reverence the pearled drops and the delicate tracery and strength of nerves and blood vessels exposed for teaching purposes. The associate professors of physiology and anatomy respectively, their mouths watering as it were, approached the beauty of the human body with passion and with awe. There was no possibility of lice of any kind.

The Professor, concerning himself in advance with endings, thinks that everything in human life and in nature has a deep psychic need for a structure of some kind. There is a need for loose ends to come together, to coincide in an agreement in some sort of order for an ending, a resolution, a satisfactory closure, in a word, for a consonance as in music, for example, the final movement, often described as the apotheosis in Beethoven's seventh symphony, supplying an extra rush of energy giving way to a deep sense of reward and fulfilment. Perhaps this might be from the rounding off of a remembered previous experience or the ending of a poem or a novel and – his thoughts blossom – the gentle but insisting penetration, the final moments in lovemaking and the warm relaxation of complete satisfaction . . . he feels he needs a platform and a lectern in order to bring the interview to an end. He notices suddenly that Dr Florence is leaning over in a strange way. She is very pale.

'That's right, dear!' The Director of Residential Management is leaping from her chair. She puts her heavy hands on the bent-over slender (and beautiful) shoulders. 'Head right down, dear, down between the knees, that's my good girl. I know it's ungainly, dear, but head right down. We're just having a little fainting fit,' the director winks at the Professor. 'Adoption,' she says, winking again. 'Adoption brings on the fainting. Many a lady has fallen pregnant while adopting, would you believe? There's been many a fainting fit in this very room. Some ladies have even gone so far as to throw up.'

Looking anxiously at Dr Florence, the Professor feels intimately responsible for her, as if his recent very personal thoughts, the very personal imaginative penetration and climactic satisfaction, closely involving himself and her, have caused her to feel disturbed and ill. He embarks, at once, on an explanation and declaration of the virginal status of his colleague whose pallor has now a greenish tinge.

'Oh! don't mind me, dear, they all say that,' the director winks again. 'The Ladies are *all* virgins.' The Professor tries not to witness another atrocious wink. Putting his arm as carefully as possible round Dr Florence to steady her on the chair, he points at the telephone.

'If I may,' he says, 'I'll phone my wife.'

'Be my guest.' The director hands over the phone.

Hazel, answering the call, says she'll be right over and will take Dr Florence and Ms Bianca home, leaving the Prof. to look after himself. Hazel will help Dr Florence to bed for a nap, Ms Bianca too, if necessary.

The Professor immediately realises he could most willingly have helped Dr Florence to bed. Her shoes would be taken off first and secondly her stockings ... He thinks of the two of them, Dr Florence and Ms Bianca, the two of them, sleeping in their nakedness, their limbs enfolded, tranquil and beautiful as in a painting by an unknown romantic artist, Viennese perhaps or possibly a Hungarian of noble blood but forever in hiding . . .

*A*doption like childbirth has its own pain and confusion. For an hour the Professor wanders in the gardens
of the university allowing himself to recover from the
interview. Dr Florence being upset has caused him to
feel distressed. It seems, all at once, that there are
many causes of distress. As he walks he recalls that he
overheard his daughters, the day before, discussing in
loud voices their mother and their aunt. It was the
general opinion that mother and aunty Chloë should
move with the times and have their chins waxed. He
was glad that, at the time, Hazel and Chloë were not
within earshot. He stepped, barefoot, from the landing
into the first bedroom where the triplets, in various
stages of undress, were examining and trying some
new cosmetics. He wandered across the thin Aubusson
carpet and, with vague gestures, drew their attention

to the tranquil view of the meadows so clear from their bedroom windows. He then said to the girls that he did not care for vulgarity. They looked at him with wide eyes and said that they did not care for it either.

Making an effort he allowed his feet the indulgence of the wooden floorboards immediately under the silkiness of the worn-out carpet. Making a further effort he changed his thoughts and, almost at once, slipped into one of his more consoling pictures, one which he sees often, that of the main office (fourth floor, sharp left from the stairwell), where the girls, or really they are women, the secretarial staff, half hidden in floral smocks and elaborate equipment, greet him when he arrives in the mornings.

Quickly they jump, fresh and lively, into any conversation which is offered, news from across the world or gossip from the campus. Laughing and telling jokes one minute and just as quickly straightening their faces into the silent appropriate sheets of paper with never a frown or a grimace at being interrupted and then discarded, left at the roadsides, so to speak, of their desks.

Without them, the Professor knows the department would be a very different place as indeed it is on those days declared as public holidays but not recognised by the university as being a part of the academic year.

Smiling to himself, sustained with recurring images of the office, he realises his walk has taken him across campus to regions unfamiliar. The soothing hour of dusk, owner of the all too reticent pinot noir, has changed into night. With a small laugh at himself, the Professor turns to walk back to the car park where the little streets of the campus, the picturesque little avenues ultimately converge, and, at that place, he will be able to find his way. At the same time he has to admit that, over recent years, the university has grown, with more buildings, beyond recognition and, in truth, he no longer knows his way about there, in the dark.

*U*nable to contemplate the difficulties in the household, the Professor allows himself a few moments of amazement before trying to put his thoughts into some kind of order. His expected role of father of the triplets in the twenty-first birthday celebrations is complicated by his distaste for the presence of the Victim (the Professor's private name for him). Distaste is hardly a part of a celebration of any kind and the Professor would like to be free from it. He is surprised that his daughters would bring home an unknown young man. He supposes their soft, innocent hearts were captured by the bandages and the extent to which he, the Victim, is encased in plaster of Paris. The amazement is over the Victim's attitude. This Victim, this young man, a complete stranger, has been given in complete generosity, at no little inconvenience to the family, the room they fondly call 'the garden sitting room', because the stairs, to one in his condition, were out of the question. This man, this unknown person, declares, at once, that he is unable to stand the William Morris wallpaper. It will, he insists then, have to be peeled off, soaked off and torn down in strips. The Professor is unable to understand how anyone, being given such hospitality, can say that the wallpaper is strangling him. And for this man to say he must have, in addition to the stripping of the walls, the removal of what he describes as overbearing and grotesque ornaments, is beyond anyone's endurance.

So far Hazel and Chloë have been outwardly silent, simply running the household and its unusual troubles with their usual competence.

The triplets, to begin with, argued and almost fought over their patient. Each one would say that *he* was *her* own *sweet* responsibility. Their voices were shrill and possessive, but are now quieter, saying as little as possible in angry hissing whispers, 'it's your turn now,' and 'it's *you* he's calling,' and '*I* took him to the bathroom last time,' reminding the Professor of the girls, years ago, home from school for the holidays, trying to avoid the simple household work of drying the dishes, mopping the floors under the beds and peeling the vegetables.

Another nuisance which cannot be spoken about is the rather private subject of the little downstairs cloakroom, a convenience regarded as being the property of the Professor. Since the multiple homecoming this very personal place is always occupied, and the Professor, unable to mention it, is disturbed and has lost his regularity. Trying to think of other things, he imagines himself as a landowner (perhaps Russian) dressed for the mornings in an elegant dressing gown with warm trimming at the neck and the wrists. Beaver, perhaps, or some other soft-furred rodent. He would then have the garden furniture brought out from the servants' quarters in readiness for the festivities.

In the absence of servants and their quarters, he will himself remember to bring down from the one-time nursery, the cane chaise longue and the matching chairs and tables. It would be pleasant, at a time like this, to be a character in a fiction. Smiling, he thinks of Thomas Mann's character, a professor who, after being helped into his heavy overcoat and his galoshes, kisses his wife, saying that he must go for his walk, and with a small click of the garden gate he sets off just as the young people are beginning to arrive for a party.

He thinks now with pleasure of his unexpected fondness for the two little boys. In comparison with his own life their lives seem so simple. He understands that this is far too simple. How can he know what complications lie ahead for any child.

He has, this evening, cleared two drawers in his desk for them. To share between them is a little pile of treasures he has put in readiness; a paper knife, some metal buttons (from an old and favourite waistcoat), a pencil sharpener in the shape of a steam engine, some picture postcards bearing foreign stamps and inscrutable messages from forgotten people, some luggage labels inscribed with exotic destinations and the hieroglyphics of examinations and permissions for travelling. In a separate heap he has put small change from different countries, the coins meaningless beyond the possibilities of identification. With tender feelings towards both children he adds new pencils and some sheets of paper (brought home from the department), to be in readiness for the expected young visitors.

He thinks fondly of the two boys and the way in which they will kneel close to his amiable legs as they find the treasures, one after the other. He looks forward to their next visit and, almost at once, reprimands himself for not anticipating, with pleasure, the forthcoming party which is an important event. He is not looking forward to it with the happiness a twenty-first birthday party for three daughters deserves.

The Professor knows that the Victim has survived a terrible accident but no one seems willing to tell him who this survivor is; and the stories of the supposed accident simply do not match each other. The conflicting descriptions tell of an avalanche and, in the same breath, explain that there was not enough snow for safe sport. The young man apparently tried to save one of the daughters and, in the attempt, had to be saved himself.

'So you see, Daddy Darling, *we* rescued *him* and

if you save a life you automatically become responsible for it – for that life.' The girls have explained that they paid this man's fare and all his expenses which means that he himself has paid; 'And if we're still counting,' he says to himself, 'as time goes by I'm still paying.'

It isn't just the money, it's something else. 'I don't even know this man's father,' he complains from time to time to Hazel and to Chloë, usually when they are out of earshot and out of sight. 'Or his mother,' he adds for the benefit of his daughters.

'He is a Victim, I'll allow for that,' he starts at breakfast as though engaging in a literary discussion with himself in the absence of students. 'But then I too am a victim and so is my wife and my sister-in-law.' He pauses, shaking a thin finger as if at someone who must be told. 'So are my daughters and so are the little orphans, we are all victims . . .'

'Oh Daddy Darling, don't be so utterly ridiculous.' A triplet is usually at his side to keep him in order. He pats the girlish arm affectionately and gives her a little kiss, with pursed lips, on her soft cheek.

Sometimes, now, he is not sure which of the

three girls is which. At one time they had clear differences, one being rather plump, another lisping slightly and the third having a lower, somewhat hoarse voice. They were all given names, pretty names from the pastoral and lyric poems taken from Greek and Roman poetry; the eclogues of Virgil, the Professor explained to Hazel and Chloë. Spencer, he said then, wrote of Phyllis, Charyllis and Amaryllis. The names of the babies suggested for him, at the time, the innocence of growing up in the woods and the meadows, playing in the fresh air and bathing in the pure waters of the streams, surrounded forever by spring flowers. But the babies became schoolgirls (boarding-school girls – handsomely from Lady Carpenter) very quickly, exactly like other girls and, all at once, were suddenly a part of suburban university campus life, exactly like other students. The Professor held on to his original pictures of them in spite of Hazel's names of the moment, Belinda, Mrs Betty or Posy, when she forgot their real names and wanted something fetched or put away quickly. Children, the Professor understood, he had to understand, grew up into ordinary, everyday people.

*I*t is a fresh morning. Rosella parrots are noisy in the flame trees. Somewhere a door slams. This slam is answered by another slam. The Professor is on his way downstairs.

Dork! another door slams. Who the hell's slamming doors. Another voice joins the first; I reckon I'm the most fucked up, like, really fucked up person in the world.

Oh! That's so sweet. Groovy.

Cool!

You're just a dork, a submissive bimbo, like I said a *bimbo*.

Hey watch it, like, just watch it.

Be with it for Chrissakes. Dyke!

Dyke, yourself.

Give it a break you two.

What's your problem, hey? We're just discussing.

You're nothing but a whatsaname an antidepressant gone wrong. You're a retard, just a tank. Move! Tank!

Get Out of My Room. Fuckin' little Bitch.

It's my room as much as yours. Get out or else . . .

Hey, where's my ring? Did you take my ring? Hey, she's got my ring. Give it back now.

Hey, my new sandals. Guess what, like, they're called 'Regardless'!

Listen you two, guess what. Last night got me hammered. I think I've lost my virginity.

Oh. Regardless of consequences, Idiot!


The door slams. The Professor pausing on the stairs does not wait to hear more. His daughters are completely changed. House too, completely changed. Scattered clothes on all the chairs and on the floors. Every mirror seems crowded with eyes and lips and strange ways with and without hair. Ever since his daughters came home there have been weepings, screamings, door slammings and tantrums over fashion, face and figure. Exotic ornaments seem to sprout from ears and noses and skin which, in the ordinary way, would be covered. Wet towels are left all over the bathroom floor and hot water is allowed to waste in the laundry . . . *Those body jewels, surely they are imitation . . .*

Days and nights are passing. The daughters and their guest have filled the house beyond expectation. The birthday celebration is now quite close. Already the Professor is putting up with offered memories and respectful tedious tributes being paid daily within the department. In addition, Cupcake and Sugarbaby (Physiology and Anatomy respectively), smiling, taking up all the space on the stairs, have alluded several times to the special day with comfortable clichéd phrases and exaggerated gestures representing the draining of innumerable imaginary wine glasses before hurling them into imaginary fireplaces. Often they count up on their now elderly fingers all the kisses they have been promised during, they say, the previous twenty-one years. The

Professor, also smiling and bowing slightly in turn, stands with determined patience during the repeated little scene.

Hazel and Chloë seem to be entirely unperturbed by the state of the household saying, above the noise of the blender and the dishwasher, things like 'you're only young once' and 'you only live once' and 'they've got all their lives ahead of them for work'. The Professor is amazed at this low level of conversation and general expression taking place in his own house. He is unable to make any sense out of Hazel and Chloë and their banal remarks.

Thanking God, under his breath, he allows himself to be sent for some sugar.

'Be a dear,' Hazel says, 'from the shop on the corner even though it's more expensive there. We're right out of sugar and we have meringues in mind.'

As he sets off, realising that he has been 'got out' of the house 'for his own good', he wishes a triplet, still tiny and delicate, would come running out after him and, putting her sticky little hand into his, would ask if she could go with him.

He hardly knows how to contain, in secret, the sadness of this hopeless and rather stupid wish. Sometimes the loneliness within the changed family, in spite of Hazel's calm good sense and her qualities as an accommodating and generous spouse, seems endless and intolerable.

He thinks of his recent wish for the sounds of excited voices all over the house which has been a silent place, except for Hazel's blender, for too long. The voices, he admits, are there but there is a great change, a change which must be partly because of the visitor, this intruder, supposedly a victim. He does not know what to think.

Feeling such thoughts to be non-profitable, especially immediately before the twenty-first celebrations, he allows himself the luxury of recalling a recent concert and the tender glance of questioning and approval passing between the solo flautist, in the orchestra, and the conductor. This glance comes when the flautist opens his eyes, after a particularly difficult and responsible passage of notes in which he is maintaining exquisite harmony with the pianist, to meet the loving and approving gaze of the Master. For the conductor, with his slender baton, has in the palm of his hand, in the movement of his shoulders and in his finger tips, the entire orchestra. But it is at this precious moment of secretly drawn breath that the flautist, after hovering in perfect restraint before giving full sound to his wordless adoration, receives the longed for single glance from *his* tutor, *his* controller and admirer – *his* master. The Professor, walking to the local shop, remembers the music and recalls that the flautist's eyelids were slightly swollen as if con- tused from the hidden but intense effort made in sustaining the performance. Mentioning this on one occasion to either Cupcake or Sugarbaby (perhaps it was to both since they are inseparable) out of curiosity, he smiles as he remembers, once more, that they had laughed (with moderation, of course), suggesting that the eyelids would not be the only swellings in the body at such times.

He understands that he owes a great deal to the wisdom of the now elderly Cupcake and Sugarbaby (it is difficult to keep their real names in mind). He remembers the first time he attended one of their joint lectures. He watched the two of them, their mouths, as always, watering as they paid homage, with reverence, to the miracle and the beauty of the human body. They moved on the platform in harmony as they spoke in turn demonstrating with a real corpse or cadaver, as they chose to call it, presented on a special table. He listened, enchanted, while various systems, organs, nerves and blood vessels were revealed and described in lyrical terms, which made their utterances into a kind of poetry quite musical in places. Similarly, a skeleton hanging in a corner was drawn forward on the stage to be matched with the tissue exposed. A poem of bones, in particular the pelvis:

the ilium, the symphysis pubis the ischium and the os innominatum help to form the pelvic girdle by the union of these bones. The acetabulum; a cup-shaped cavity on the external surface of the bone – receives the head of the femur in the formation of the hip joint . . .

Strangely he remembers the names of the bones though he is aware that, over the years, some names have been changed. He remembers that when traces of disease were discovered in the liver, the only thing he could do was to leave as silently as possible, bent double, through a small side exit reserved, of course, for the corpse.

Later, Cupcake, having noticed his retreat, explained that the dissection of the cadaver, whether healthy or diseased or even simply worn out in old age, was on the same level as the coming to an understanding of a well-written literary work by intelligent reading and discussion.

The Professor had, at the time and ever since, been grateful for this analogy. A parallel to be offered at the suburban dinner table or, of course, to students.

Inadvertently he has walked on beyond the shop. He returns and buys the sugar and walks home. A combination of the walk, the fresh air and his thoughts have made him feel better. That is so like Hazel. She is wise. He hopes he is never in a position of deceit in which he would not want to see Hazel coming towards him. He holds in his mind, forever he hopes, an image of Hazel and Chloë together, side by side, standing like two mature pears, golden in a shaft of late afternoon sunlight, at the end of the kitchen table, smiling their serene greetings on his daily returnings from the university.

Sometimes he is aware that his reverence and admiration, his *fondness* for Dr Florence and his tender understanding of her needs, could exceed the boundaries of his vivid imagination and cause an all too easily imagined unhappiness to become a painful reality from which there would be no turning away, no escape for any one of them.

Perhaps there even can be something said in favour of the distraction, the sheer nuisance of the presence of the Victim and the surprisingly hurtful changes in the behaviour and the temperaments of the triplets. Bad behaviour, he remembers reading, is often the result of a deep unhappiness. He must keep this in mind. But more importantly, he must try to think of ways in which to alleviate the troubles in the household.

'Catch you later,' he hears the Director of Residential Management once more in the memory of their parting on the steps of St Monica's. The breathless farewell remembered brings once more to his mind the solemn faces of the two little boys. He can see all over again their crooked spectacles and their youthful chubby knees. He supposes he could have replied to the director's meaningless phrases with a quotation, his expression serious and one finger poised in readiness to seal his lips.

*Melancholy* PAUSE, for finger on lips, *is the nurse of frenzy*

and

*Therefore they thought it good to hear a play*
*And frame your mind to mirth and merriment*
*which bars a thousand harms and lengthens life.*

Bad behaviour, the Professor remembers reading, is often the result of deep unhappiness. It is all too easy to simply sense the overpowering effect of a large family and the tremendous responsibility involved. The whole problem has to be faced in the best way possible. The loneliness of the 'only' child (himself, he thinks, for Delia, his twin, spent her childhood in an exclusive boarding school, going on to a finishing school in Switzerland) is in reality only a small part of the loneliness of being a *small part* in a large family. The quarrels and the teasings and the impatience for strictly small but really essential things like the bathroom, for instance, can wound and scar the most easily disposed (in personality) child for life.

His mother, Lady Carpenter, had remarked one time after a weekend at her son's house, that she was completely unable to understand how two people, Hazel and her sister Chloë, could remain so unmarked. *Their faces*, she said then, and *their expressions*, she couldn't understand how they remained *so unmarked*. She, herself, after just two days of the family life, had developed deep lines and wrinkles in her skin *and* a peculiar haunted look in her eyes. Also her inguinal hernia, usually untroubled and quiet, had gone into spasm. It had been a mistake, she explained then, for her to make her visit when the girls were at home for their half-term holidays.

She had come to the understanding that Hazel and Chloë were completely devoid of anything selfishly sexual in their appearance or in their speech and demeanour; their faces being unravished by desire or jealousy or anger, in fact there was nothing horrid or mean (Lady Carpenter's own words) about either of them. She had meant, on occasion, to question as to where and how her son met these two women in the first place. They were not 'university', she declared, they had no greasy hair bands, no shoddy flapping footwear and certainly did not give the impression of dowdy, grubby, unevenly hemmed tweeds, a recognisable habit of the female Don at Oxford. Surely he must recall, remember, these women.

She had, she said, no recollection of him (her son) telling her or explaining how he came to marry them, for it really did seem that he had married them both. Two angels, she said, two accommodating angels, very plain angels but who, she said, is questioning?

'An accommodating wife,' Lady Carpenter said to herself on the short journey to the railway station, 'spouse is a better word, an accommodating spouse and similar sister-in-law'.

Hazel and Chloë, in the back seats, were planning a marathon in marmalade, the Seville oranges having been noticed in the market, and did not hear the farewell mutterings of their recent visitor.

The Professor, preparing in his mind, *the soft anvil, beloved of the poets*, for his afternoon class, heard the music of his mother's voice. As so often happens with a well-known hymn from childhood, he rested in the familiar harmony of sound and did not bother to cherish the sacred words.

Another cool Sunday morning. The doves are calling and murmuring across the gardens. A spring-hatched magpie, refusing to grow up and be responsible, is following the mother bird, uttering cries of distress which the Professor thinks must be uncomfortable for this mother.

Remembering his own mother from previous

visits he realises that he has her way of reading the countenance of someone with whom he might be sitting or walking. He understands that this precludes easily anything the companion might actually be thinking or saying, because in his close and silent reading of the facial expression, he is often putting his own opinions and discourse into the other, simply from his own sensibility and his own private, unspoken readings regardless of what might be in the other's thoughts.

Over the years it has comforted him to feel that he pays attention and responds, because there is no other way, to Dr Florence, to her every thought and need. He has told her on every possible occasion, when they have a moment alone, that though he is husband and father, he does have a very special love for her. He takes care to tell her that he needs her intensely and that he will never stop being grateful for her feelings about him. They smile knowing, because they have told each other, that they have sweet and gentle smiles which enhance their faces. He knows within himself that he is aware of every change, every delicate emotion and every thought and feeling in Dr Florence's expression. He allows himself the unkind thought that, on the other hand, Ms Bianca's face reminds him of a turnip hollowed out for All Saints' Eve and illuminated by an overpowering coarse candle. He stops at that point, knowing that he should not indulge in schoolboy thoughts, such thoughts being unprofitable.

All the same it is a long time for both of them, Dr Florence and himself, to be secretly in love, to love each other and to have to be apart.

The two women are quite likely to choose to go off somewhere together or, if they feel like it, to stay at home secluded in their small apartment even when they have 'ongoing' invitations from Hazel. He understands that certain outward appearances have to be maintained.

On this cool Sunday morning Dr Florence is pale and fragile. Ms Bianca, in contrast, has a tight-skinned redness as if from a recent and unadmitted face job. She is patting both fiery cheeks with fingertips, orange from some special lubricating ointment. Hazel and

Chloë, in order to avoid disappointing the boys, have fetched them from the residential college. The Professor is sitting on the terrace with his coffee, watching the boys as they wash the car with the garden hose. With some awkwardness they were persuaded to take off their cotton jumpers and to put on some old shirts to keep their own clothes clean.

Hazel explained that they would keep their clothes folded on a chair ready for their return to St Monica's.

The lawn mower has been pulled from the shed and placed in a sunny spot to encourage the motor to start easily.

The boys have not really spoken except to say, 'Good morning, sir,' to the Professor in scarcely audible voices.

'Heavens! The ZOO, how too awful! I, we can't possibly go to the zoo today.' Dr Florence and Ms Bianca retreat at once from the idea of entertaining their twins. In the face of these outraged feelings Hazel and Chloë are silent. They take their kneelers and their gardening gloves and, giving the twins an approving wave, they continue where they left off the evening before.

Now, as she is on her knees, weeding round the Professor's chair, Hazel points out, with her usual wisdom, that simply coming to the house every weekend would be too much like being cooped up in Saint Monica's without the benefit of the occasional little treats which could well be an organised part of the orphanage life.

'Books and music are all very nice,' Hazel says, 'but these boys need a farm with cows and hens to go to, or they should be taken to the beach.' The Professor, remembering their own family outings, shudders, but he has to agree. Hazel is, as always, absolutely right. Thoughtfully he watches her being drawn away by her weeds. He reflects on the story of Monica, the mother of Augustine. Saint Augustine renowned for his love of the simple pleasures:

*I can distinguish the scent of lilies from that of violets even though there is no scent at all in my nostrils, and simply*

*by using my memory I recognize that I like*
*honey better than wine . . .*
*All this goes on inside me, in the vast cloisters*
*of my memory . . .*

'Perhaps I should tell the boys the story of Saint Augustine,' the Professor suggests to Hazel as she weeds her way towards him once more, 'and of his mother.'

'Perhaps,' Hazel replies with a touch of doubt in her voice. 'Perhaps while we have tea . . . at tea time?'

The sound of the lawn mower fills the afternoon. Chloë must have managed to get the obstinate creature going. Filled with admiration for Chloë's muscles, the Professor notices that the boys take turns with the machine. For a moment he allows himself the rather disloyal but pleasurable feeling of luxury as he remembers the all too frequent screamings of the triplets when all three, forever it seemed, wanted the same toy, the same book, the same dress and even the lawn mower at one and the same time. Life is far more peaceful with these twins whose home, in spite of its elaborate name, is an orphanage. He has read somewhere of the subdued level of living observed in children growing up in an institution. However kindly they are approached and spoken to, they are more subdued than children who are being brought up in individual homes with their own fathers and mothers. He watches the bigger twin helping the smaller one to guide the machine. He hopes they won't mow each other's feet. Craning his neck, nervously, he can see that Chloë has provided them both with thick socks and solid old gardening shoes.

Dr Florence and Ms Bianca, nursing their head-aches, and with profuse apologies, have gone home to their shared apartment. The Professor can never quite rid himself of small twinges of envy whenever he, at times like this, imagines the intimate Sunday afternoon which, he is certain, will reward and restore them both completely. This completeness, he has read about it, is the gift of love. Especially he thinks about love between women and that it is a real and powerful demonstration. In considering the delicate and endless caress, he enfolds Dr Florence in the sweetness and fragrance of Tennyson's 'immortal flower of legend', and the 'sacred herb of mystical power', as if Dr Florence can be, in this way, both beloved and protected at the same time. He does not trust Ms Bianca at all. Dismissing her, he places Dr Florence, her smooth back and shoulders, her long straight thighs, her small but perfect breasts, all the perfect fashioning of her imagined nakedness, *propt on beds of amaranth and moly*, on a fragrant bank of soft grass and flowers; preferably hyacinths, even though he is aware that the university apartments have only small, flat squares of shaved grass and shared concrete paths which are swept by one of the more industrious groundsmen.

In his private picture of the lovers there is no anxiety, no thought of failure in the wished for satisfaction. The culmination of the slowly mounting passion and the accompanying sensations are assured in advance in the serenity of their known expectations. Overhearing snatches of conversation one time in the corridor, he heard that a woman's love for another woman was 'cool'. He understands that anything 'cool' is 'all right'.

At tea time the Professor is relieved that the long drawn-out Sunday is moving towards the evening.

'Saint Monica,' he tells the twins while they are eating Hazel's fruit loaf, 'Saint Monica was the mother of Saint Augustine but they were not always saints. Augustine's mother wept so much over the dissolute habits of her son she was made into a saint. She was *canonised* and this means she was admitted to the calendar of saints . . .'

The twins, nicely washed and brushed by Chloë, are sitting close together politely eating whatever is passed to them. The Professor, waving a delicate hand and holding his tea cup with the other, explains that Monica was regarded as a tiresome mother and Augustine was not a gentle, kind son. A certain bishop, he goes on to explain, made the legendary remark that it was impossible that the child of so much weeping should be discarded. Augustine, the Professor brings his explanation to a close, had many difficult and painful experiences and he realised, in time, that his mother was to be highly regarded, that is, the Professor says, Augustine realised in time that he loved his mother and she loved him. Both became saints, the secret in human life being endurance and determination.

The Professor, during the silence at the garden table while Hazel is fetching chocolate biscuits and Chloë *and* the refilled tea pot from the kitchen, asks the boys what they are reading now. Do they read any Shakespeare in class? he asks them. In the continuing silence he remembers a visiting Shakespeare scholar saying that all boys and girls of eight to ten years should be thrown into the audience of a Shakespearean production. The magic, the scholar said then, would take hold, would seize the children, offering them thought-provoking realism as well as enchantment forever. Would the twins, he asks them in the extended silence, would they like to accompany him and his wife to a play? Chloë would, of course, be joining them as well, he hastens to add. The play would be *The Taming of the Shrew*, he explains. He looks at the twins who are, in their shyness, unable to meet his kind and enthusiastic gaze. The Professor then recalls, for his guests, a performance several years earlier of this play – in modern dress. Though faithful to Shakespeare it was a contemporary production. 'There was a motor car on stage,' he warms to his subject, 'can you imagine a motor car on the stage?' He goes on to describe the two sisters, dressed in white artificial silk, in princess slips with opera tops of lace, throwing their Mason Pearson hair brushes at each other . . . He pauses, understanding all at once, that these boys would not be able to place this description anywhere in their thoughts of remembered experience. He has offered them images, recalled happily for himself, belonging to a specific time years ago and quite beyond their imaginative reach.

'Have some more cake,' he passes the plate. 'Come along, eat up! It has to be eaten otherwise I shall have to eat stale cake all the week.' He realises immediately that this burdensome picture he has given of himself might seem to be a glimpse of an enviable life, adding acutely to their own unenviable orphaned lives.

Fortunately there is rescue, in the shape of Hazel and Chloë coming across the lawns. Hazel suggests that the two boys, their hands full of biscuits, might like to explore the garden and the various sheds while the grown ups finish off the tea pot and clear up the tea things before driving back to Saint Monica's.

The Professor, being frequently occupied with intellectual reasoning, is often perplexed in his purpose of action and this afternoon he carries, singly, a plate and a saucer and puts them on the ironing board. He returns to the garden tea table for another plate only to find that, between them, Hazel and Chloë have stacked up the empty plates and cups and saucers, the tea pot, the milk jug and the sugar bowl and cleared the whole lot in one journey. On going to his study to look up more accurate details about the story of Saint Monica, he remembers that in the various writings about the saints there are many overlapping or contradictory details and very little authentic material. Many saints, Madeleine for one, were educationalists. In general it was thought that women who became saints had been educated and perhaps influenced by elder brothers. And if his memory is correct, almost all the women endured hardship and suffering. They wept a great deal, not necessarily for themselves, but as if carrying all the burdens and sorrows of human life. In books written about the lives of the saints, writers seem to have resorted to relying on previous accounts rather as recipes are copied and written down with similarities and small changes every time.

Walking back, without pursuing further useful information, to his comfortable, well-placed garden chair, he knows that he has not enough reliable material for delivery. He wishes that he could think of a suitable joke or some riddles for the boys. He feels that he has been a very dull and inadequate host.

Slowly the Professor walks on towards the bottom of the garden. His thoughts are troublesome. They, himself, Chloë and Hazel, have started on something which will either have to be ended immediately or continued with a deeply felt fondness and enthusiasm. It was like a three-cornered love affair in a novel or even, of course, a similar triangle as in real life. A decision was essential.

The enthusiasm will have to be genuine and loving. It seems that Dr Florence alone will not have the freedom, the demands of Ms Bianca have always to be considered first. And, more seriously, Dr Florence does seem, at present, to be lacking in energy. He stands still, staring at the little heaps of mown grass. This lack of energy could mean that Dr Florence was unhappy, deeply unhappy. He moves on towards the vegetable plots and the sheds. He pauses. He can hear a rough boyish voice singing in the shed. It is the partly broken voice of the elder twin. The Professor smiles at the idea of the elder one singing to the younger one. The boy is catching his breath as if trying to subdue his voice, as if trying not to make too much noise. All at once the Professor understands that the child is crying and, at the same time, is trying not to cry, there in the dark corner of the shed. He can hear the younger boy's voice, shrill, the voice of a little boy still, begging the older brother not to cry.

Peering, the Professor can see the elder twin crouched in the darkness, his face hidden in both hands. The younger twin, seeing the Professor, tries again to hush his brother's grief.

'Is it because we didn't go to the zoo today?' The

Professor, with reverence in the face of such despair, asks his question in a low voice. 'Is it because we didn't go to the zoo?' Images of the zoo flood his mind. Only a few weeks ago a visiting professor, to the department, had expressed a wish to see a koala bear. The visit took place on a very hot morning after a hot night. The dingoes were lying in the dust, that day, like thrown-out door mats, a crocodile sulked in a small pool and the monkeys, usually energetic, were silent, sitting with their backs to each other and towards the visitors suggesting a reflection of suburban boredom and loneliness, the epitome of depression, all too well known, and which has simply to be endured. Of course the sought after bears were rolled up, their faces hidden, looking like disreputable greyish bath towels high up, almost out of sight, in the topmost branches of the tall eucalypts . . .

'Is it because we didn't go to the zoo today? Is that why you are so upset?' The Professor is bending over trying to draw the twins out of their huddled distress.

The bigger twin, his plump face red and swollen

with crying, tries to melt into the back of the shed.

'No, it's not because of the zoo,' the smaller twin says, 'he's crying because . . .'

'Go on,' says the Professor, 'you can tell me.'

'He's crying,' the smaller twin explains, 'he's crying because he thought . . . well he was hoping that our mother would be coming here, you know, that our mother would be coming back for us.'

Hardly able to bear the pain of this, and helpless without Hazel and a suitable quotation, the Professor puts his hand on the boy's thick shoulder. And then bending down, and steadying himself, he encircles the child with his arm. He lowers himself on to a large upturned flower pot and draws both boys, both are weeping now, to himself, as if with a slight rocking movement, he is able to draw all lost and alone children and their mothers close to his heart.

He has no parallel for this. He has no answer.

*Seeing too much sadness hath congealed my blood . . .* Knowing that he is probably misquoting, the Professor, having previously no quotation, is relieved to be able to say the words, almost in a crooning tone, as if in a nursery rhyme, an antidote to counteract the pain of disappointment. *Melancholy is the nurse of frenzy mirth and merriment:* the Professor, still holding the boys and rocking, repeats the words as if singing to the two children, a cradle song, a song of consolation; *frame your mind to mirth and merriment which bars a thousand harms . . .* as in the chanting of nursery rhymes he sings as if groaning the words over and over, his voice almost disappearing and then returning.

At last Hazel appears, filling the doorway of the shed. She has two little parcels of homemade biscuits for the boys to take back with them.

They all walk back over the freshly mown grass. Hazel suggests that, on their next visit, they can learn how to bake biscuits. As they walk, the smaller twin holds the Professor's hand. He would like, he tells the Professor, he thinks they both, his brother and himself, would like to watch a play. The lion-taming one, he says, the one that Sir was telling them about a little while ago.

It was extraordinary, the Professor turns his thoughts over, *extraordinary* how the child had made an image for himself between the few casual words dropped upon his ears and an immensity of incorrect understanding.

In the car Hazel explains about the forthcoming twenty-first birthday party. Would the boys like to come? she asks them. They could come to the party and sleep over, if they liked the idea, in a little tent on the lawn.

'Oh What Fun!' Chloë says.

'Yes, it will be fun,' Hazel agrees.

The Professor driving slowly, in a leisurely way, one hand only on the steering wheel, can see that the two of them, Hazel and Chloë, are trying to surround the two youthful owners of grief with fun, lots and lots, in Chloë's way and in Hazel's way, lots of it. Great fun, they say.

'Great fun!' the Professor adds to the creation of the fun.

What does it matter, the Professor goes over his

thoughts, if the little boy misunderstood his reference to *The Taming of the Shrew*. Vaguely he considers the possibility of a visiting circus coming some time. Even if he himself (and certainly Dr Florence) do not care for the circus, he can rely on Hazel and Chloë. He will ask Hazel.

In the meantime the Shakespeare might well be a spectacular and unforgettable experience for the twins . . .

The fuckin' bitch!

She's a total mutant.

What a tank, yeah, a tank.

Yeah, needs hammering.

She's working the lawns. Oh, look at that willya.

She's right into it.

Yeah, Bitch. You can see it all . . . total misfits.

Close the window and the curtain willya.

They can see right into us . . .


The Professor, helping Lady Carpenter on the stairs, hopes his mother is unable to hear the flattering remarks. The daughters are dressing and, changing their minds, undressing all over the house as they have done since they were big enough to dress themselves.

Do me up, Daddy, down the back, do me up, I can't reach.

Daddy, I can't find my other sandal. Daddy, find my sandal.

Daddy, I am not wearing these. These knickers they *show* under my party dress. Daddy, I won't wear them!

He seems to hear their little girl voices all over the house. Tender memories come back to him. Everything is different now. His daughters' remarks about their friends seem to him to be unnecessarily unkind.

How on earth, Lady Carpenter wants to know as they reach the hall, how on earth had Hazel and Chloë managed to give up gathered waists, frills, puff sleeves, spotted material and reversible embroidered satin ribbons? She supposes that Hazel will have given away (possibly Hazel's own words?) the block bodice, that foundation for all their homemade clothes. Surely the pattern would not be needed for those ridiculous bits of cloth stuck at random on their bodies, 'the daughters' bodies, of course!' The Professor and his mother pause for breath. Though he does not want to speak of it in front of her, he is as surprised as she is to see his daughters 'featured' (their word) in the fashion pages of the women's magazines. He has never, completely, been able to understand what was meant by modelling. The girls, *his triplets*, in the coloured photographs, are half-naked strangers. Their faces are altered in length with pouting lips drawn down as if with discontent. Their eyes are no longer innocent, their gaze being one of troubled emptiness. They offer only a stare of indifference instead of a smile or a burst of happy laughter. They, the girls, in every movement of their bodies and with every word they speak, seem to be the bearers of deceitfulness.

Their fragments of clothing are simply patches of coloured cloth on their smooth bare skin, the coloured bandages (the only word to describe them) flattening their breasts. Their tiny panties are flesh-coloured and creased, the shadows giving an impression of nakedness and that morsel of the anatomy so revered by John Wilmot (poet), Earl of Rochester . . .

'I was never enthusiastic,' Lady Carpenter admits while accepting a fourth glass of port, 'about the gels' dedication, at school, to the drawing and endless colouring of pretty maps. Their excellent marks were, I grant you, for their looks, with the maps being second only to their long handsome thighs, their regular features and their shining hair, *and* they had such engagin' smiles.'

The Professor knows that he has to agree. The awful part is that he knows, as well, that the maps meant nothing, apart from their prettiness, to the triplets. They have returned from their travelling without any idea at all that they visited, or could have visited, some of the beauty spots marked so lovingly in coloured inks in the series of decorative pages on display in the classroom.

Facing his disappointment in the hard fact that his daughters have not been changed or improved by their travelling, as he had hoped they would be, the Professor allows himself to remember the powerful grip the majestic mountains had put on his own youthful imagination. He has never forgotten his first visit to the mighty mountain ranges in the heart of the *Bernese Oberland*. He feels that he would like to tell someone about the height of these mountains, and about the little railway which now makes travelling easier but still magical. *Grindelwald* he wants to say is . . . and the *Jungfraujoch*, he leaps in thought, the *Jungfraujoch* is called 'the maiden' in honour of an order of nuns. Then there is the *Mönch* (an easier climb) 'the Monk'. He is unable to recall at the moment the third name, *Finster* something . . . and his thoughts and memories rush to the Ice Palace and the famous glacier walk to the *Konkordiaplatz*. Surely all this is as popular now as it was when he was a young man. Hazel would remember the name of the highest mountain, something like *Finsteraarhorn*. But his mother is waiting to leave. After telling Hazel and Chloë that they must do something about their brindled and bushy hair, 'that is if you have any hair left after this ridiculous and extravagant party'.

And forgetting to leave her wildly wrapped presents for the triplets, Lady Carpenter asks to have her car brought round into the kitchen yard.

The Professor, together with the chauffeur, manages to stow his mother in the back seat of the car. He later comforts himself with the frugal pleasure in his daughters' backpacking that they did 'do' India pretty thoroughly. One had only to count the items of very odd jewellery, especially the 'pieces' for the ears, the nose, the tongue, the navel and the nipples.

$B$ecause the party will not be starting till eight o'clock, or even nine, Hazel says that the little boys can put themselves to bed in their tent as soon as they feel tired.

The Professor wishes for his bed. For some reason he feels nervous, agitated, worried, he finds all these words applicable. As well as the expected friends of the triplets, various guests, colleagues from the department and others from the university, Sugarbaby and Cupcake, Professor Lieberman (Music), the emeritus professors of Maths and Political Economics and many others, including the women from the office, are invited. It is all rather a responsibility – being the father of triplets now twenty-one years old – *and* having a party.

The triplets, since their first hours in their little

regulation cots, have been known about and worshipped by a number of respectable acquaintances.
Some of these having been overcome with surprise and
curiosity that the girls, daughters of a highly regarded
academic and a woman well known for her practical
good sense and unquestionable moral attitudes *and* a
bird watcher as well, should have become fashion man-
nequins, all three of them mixing with the haute
couture and with the live models of ordinary dress-
makers to say nothing of *others* hanging on to the thin
edges of the clothing industry – 'industry' being a
slightly better word than trade or the clothing and
fashion world.

The surprise and curiosity had come first over
the fact that the Prof. and Hazel between them could
have produced these daughters. One child would have
been surprise enough, but *three* and 'such lovely girls'
was the unrefusable invitation to visit, to keep in
touch, to speculate on these beautiful and gifted
creatures and to keep the family 'under observation'.
Campus life has many hazards and competitive watch-
fulness has often been at the top of the list.

All the invitations to the twenty-first celebration were accepted by return post, and some even more immediately by telephone.

'The food alone will be worth going for,' guests in anticipation remarked as the special day came nearer. They reminded each other about the contents of the cellar, stored carefully all these years. And on this important occasion guests would be required to share and appreciate. It was only natural.

And there will be other guests; Dr Florence, because of her marking, will be coming later. Ms Bianca is sure to be coming as well as the young people whose names the Professor either has forgotten or never known. Already this evening there was an eager young man in a raincoat in the hall. The Professor, reminded of someone he knew, told him to make himself comfortable, suggesting that he put his equipment (it looked like surveying tripods) in the downstairs cloakroom if the Resident Teddy Bear (a little joke coming quickly to the Professor's mind) did not object to the bundle of 'golf sticks' being foisted upon him.

The coloured lights are in graceful festoons in the trees and the bushes. The band is warming up with some rather offensive sounds. The Professor has not forgotten the rattan furniture. It is much shabbier than he remembers. Bits of it are arranged in places where he imagines guests might want to sit down. Sounds of laughter and of crying and the slamming of at least two bedroom doors reassure him that the triplets are actually dressing.

The drummer has brought, he says, entering the sanctuary of the study, a little half-million dollar 'poil necklace'. *'Thrown together'* it is and would the Prof. like to have it cheap? A lovely door prize for a lovely lady, perhaps a wife and mother? Could the Prof. refuse such an offer! For a very lovely lady, very feminine, 'very emotional jewels poils' are, and a very special price for the gentleman, father of three beautiful daughters, 'el cheepo don't', he insists, 'do not miss the chance of a lifetime.'

The Professor, seeing in his worried state three pairs of hands trying to grab the pearls, sending them scattered from their broken string, is embarrassed.

'You like to make me an offer?' The drummer should never have been allowed to enter the study. The Professor supposes there was no one present to prevent the audacious entrance. He makes conventional shoulder-shrugging movements and almost succeeds in turning his pockets inside out. He adds all the well-known body language demonstrating his poverty, saying that he is completely broke, using phrases which are not natural to him. At the same time he is able to see, from the drummer's point of view, that there must be money about somewhere in order to have a band and himself, the drummer, functioning at such a large celebration.

The drummer, unexpectedly sulking later, produces some sinister drum rollings which he insists are merely practice in readiness for the evening. The Professor is already afraid that the music will penetrate beyond his walls and hedges and disturb the neighbours.

The Professor, though dressed for the evening, is without shoes or slippers. The two little orphans are pushing a shoe and a slipper each over the polished floorboards. They are playing a game called 'Buses'. There are little groups of tiny china animals, pencils, small ornaments, including an ash tray, waiting by table and chair legs for the buses to come by. These 'passengers' are picked up, moved on and set down. It seems a childish game for the boys but the Professor finds the sounds of their engines and the inventions of dialogue, given to the occupants of the buses, relaxing.

He blows up a few more balloons. There can never be too many balloons at a birthday party especially if it is a party for three, for triplets.

'Where's the Victim?' the irritation is heard easily in the Professor's voice. 'Where's our little flower, our Narcissus, our self-appointed Adonis, our Dandy? I don't suppose, by any chance, he's gone? Really gone? Perhaps Venus called?'

'Ms Bianca might be with him. She's been spending a lot of time with him lately,' Hazel says in an ordinary voice as if commenting on unchanging weather conditions. The Professor knows that Hazel is not capable of insinuating gossip.

'She came early,' Hazel went on, 'to help in the kitchen but disappeared almost immediately. Quite two of a pair, aren't they.'

The Professor has never ceased to admire Hazel's ability to create utter platitudes out of nothing. Chloë has the same comfortable gift but is more inclined to provide an echo to the most banal words and phrases before Hazel has finished uttering them.

'The present remarks are enlightening but not enlightening enough,' the Professor replies, feeling as if he is trying to encourage a Master's student during a one-to-one discussion.

The evening seems to pass slowly. The older guests have come with their presents and birthday kisses for the girls. And, after a drink in the kitchen with Hazel and Chloë, have taken their coloured balloons and the pretty little packages of birthday cake and moved on to the theatre or a dinner invitation, somewhere as far away from a twenty-first birthday party as possible. The Professor conducting Cupcake and Sugar and their wives to the front door envies them, their evening at the Music Lovers' Society, in spite of knowing that the program is not Schubert but something contemporary and hardly bearable. Last month a man's voice, during a page-turning pause in the song cycle, was heard clearly expressing something more than mere approval – *She carries her size well* – for a singer generously enriched with fat. The fat singer in the previous Music Lovers' evening regaled (the only way to describe it) them with a medley from *Annie Get Your Gun* and a couple of numbers (her description) from a revival of *Bless the Bride*. The Professor, greatly disappointed at the time, feels quite prepared to undergo the same music rather than the present anxiety. He thinks, lovingly, of a quiet evening with these colleagues and their wives and, of course, Hazel's cooking. He waits in the hall, more guests are sure to appear soon.

Recently there was some brain surgery on television. An old man had a disease removed from his brain by laser. It would be interesting to know, he thinks, if Sugarbaby and Cupcake, in their professional status, kept up with modern medicine and surgery alongside their teaching of anatomy and physiology as he himself felt obliged to be familiar with post-colonial writing and, for example, the experimental and the science-fiction writing. A discussion would be, to say the least, soothing.

During an interminable lull he revisits the kitchen where he decants more port. 'Twenty-one years ago,' he reminds Hazel and Chloë, 'this port was put down in the cellar.' He pours himself a glass and allows his sensitive nose to appreciate the fine quality. He pours for Hazel and Chloë and they raise their glasses, smiling towards each other and then towards him.

Some guests arrive at last. Young women with high-pitched screams and laughter. They rush upstairs with the triplets.

'It's all right, Daddy,' Amaryllis calls out, 'we're going to try on each other's drag.'

The Professor, watching, is surprised at the plain narrow black dresses, slashed, revealing long thin legs, smooth shoulders, vulnerable ribs and the now, apparently, fashionable breastbone. His daughters, in particular, appear to be anorexic, their big black ankle boots being responsible for this self-created image.

There is no sign of Ms Bianca or of the Incubus, a *Pocket Oxford Dictionary* name for the Victim. Perhaps the Victim, the Incubus, has been overpowered by a selection of carved elephants and suffocated by William Morris. It is the kind of thing which could happen. It is like being bitten by a dog when the dog senses that you are afraid of dogs. The Professor, knowing that ornaments become trivial in the passing glance of one who does not appreciate them, spares a passing thought for the insults suffered by his treasures, in particular the signs of the Zodiac, silver pressed in ebony, a sort of shield, and three life-size baby heads of the triplets, sculpted in local clay, and bronzed by either the wife of Cupcake or was it Sugarbaby? He is not able to remember which lady is or was the sculptress. Immediately he recalls the one-time art student, studying anatomy for her sculpting, and falling deliciously in love with her lecturer and marrying him. Sugarbaby's wife, of course, she is responsible for the baby heads.

The house is very quiet with the triplets and their special guests shut away in a bedroom. A few more young women have arrived and are standing at the edge of the lawn. Seeing them from the upstairs landing window, the Professor goes down to them to shake hands and to give them a run-down on the weather forecast for the evening.

As if the Professor's handshake has given a secret sign, the band strikes up. The drum beat and the powerful saxophone make it possible to imagine that crowds of people are having a wonderful time dancing.

The volume swells, the surrounding neighbours, surely feeling left out, must be envious of those invited to the celebration.

'Music expresses thoughts and wishes for which there are no adequate words'; the Professor reminds himself of a fragment of conversation should he need something to say; 'Music expresses thoughts and wishes . . .'

The little group of girls, the shy daughters of colleagues and friends from the triplets' school days, have taken the liberty of sitting down on the rattan chairs, drawing them into little circles of concentrated shyness and partly hidden anxieties about clothes. The

Professor wishes he had thought of some nice remarks to make about their dresses. Instead, remembering the pleasure his first-year students have in discovering the human element in the ancient myths and legends, an example being the *Electra* of Euripides, he describes for the girls the passage in the text in which Aegistus leaps and dances on Agamemnon's grave. He offers to go indoors to fetch the text to read to them so that they may hear the poetry and enjoy, in imagination, the scene. And, more particularly, the powerful dialogue between Electra and her mother, words of painful truth which exist still between mothers and daughters at the present time.

Hazel calls to ask if some food should be put back to keep warm, she reminds that reheated food must be properly reheated; the Professor hears Chloë's little echo, 'properly reheated'.

'Electra must wait,' he tells the guests, 'supper is about to be served.'

The triplets are, with their special guests, still upstairs altering their clothes and their hair. He runs lightly upstairs and, opening the first door, is greeted with little screams.

'Supper is ready,' he reminds gently and runs back downstairs.

There is no sign of the Victim or of Ms Bianca. Dr Florence has not yet arrived. The Victim is not in his special garden-bed-sitting room. And his wheelchair is not parked, as it so often is, by the downstairs cloakroom.

In the kitchen Hazel and Chloë are stranded, cut off from everyone by the heavily laden kitchen table. They are arranging more food which has been delivered by handsome young men on motorcycles. These young men, the Professor almost tells them, they would be better off using their time to study their lecture notes on the consonance of an ancient play or a well-written contemporary novel. They could have an amusing discussion making comparisons between the consonance in literature and the consonance in music.

With light steps he takes a tray laden with finger food for the band, chicken legs in foil, crispy fried prawns, cheese triangles and smoked salmon on flaps of Turkish bread.

The Professor, trying in what he believes to be contemporary language, tells himself to 'get himself together' and to 'get the party off the ground'. He is suddenly confronted by members of the band who tell him they are vegetarians and that they don't drink alcohol, especially port wine, they do not drink!

Chloë reaches, with her muscles, into the freezer for a spinach quiche, and Hazel puts out a jug of iced water. The Professor, relieved, steps into the protection of his own thoughts and his wishes for Dr Florence to arrive. Or rather he wishes to slip away from the nightmare of the scattered guests who do not seem to know any party behaviour, especially the triplets and their special guests. Every time he goes upstairs there is water rushing in the bathroom and, once, when he leans into the open window on the landing to rest, a conversation drifts upwards to his unwilling ears.

'There's a heap of top drawer tottie right here,' he hears the drawling voice of a young man on the path immediately below the window. 'Let's go and get us some chicks to sex up with.' The Professor flinches at the appalling language.

'Yeah!' the other voice speaks. 'Yeah, I'm right with yas. Could handle some girlie bonding right now.'

'Come on,' the first voice says, 'this way to serious cunt territory.'

'Yeah, I'm right in whenever you say the word.'

'Yeah, Hot Tottie, here we come!'

The Professor, shocked by the overheard conversation, is not sure whether he is shocked even more by his secret listening from the window above the side path. It is certainly difficult to get this party 'off the ground', not his words really. He is anxious about Dr Florence. He is worn out with waiting for her to come.

Remembering Flaubert's cab drive and his own wished for version of this escape, the passion, the designs and the plans for erotic sensuous pleasure are all in the imagination . . . and he is relieved that this is so, merely a metaphorical escape towards stolen and forbidden wishes and sensations.

After such an experience he would be unable to

welcome the sight of Hazel coming towards him, smiling, with Chloë beside her.

Not wanting the company of your wife is quite unthinkable. Living in such circumstances would bring an incurable unhappiness, and might even hasten a fatal illness of some sort. He knows that this kind of thing can happen and he is not able to speak to anyone about it.

He longs for the arrival of Dr Florence. Just to see her and have her near him would be enough. His feeling for her and wishing for her are intense. Something must have happened to keep her away.

The disappearance of the Victim and Ms Bianca adds to the strangeness. The whole evening is like a bad dream, especially as the band has broken out once more with a vocal called 'Spiritual Noise' and a piece called 'Nausea'.

Hazel and Chloë at the end of the kitchen table seem as if nothing can disturb their serenity. They seem to be entirely unaware of his unhappiness, his anguish over the ways in which the party is failing. It is not their fault that they stand so firmly established in what is to them their right place. Because of this rightness of place and himself without, it seems, any place, he feels irritated beyond words. When the two orphans come into the kitchen for their supper, he overloads their plates with cold meats and pickles and, distractedly, pats their heads; and, pulling a whole bunch of balloons down, pushes them both out into the garden. He is aware of Hazel frowning.

Feeling suddenly ashamed and tired, he goes slowly upstairs. He knocks once more on the bedroom doors, in turn, asking his daughters in a tender and, he thinks, treacherous soft voice, to come downstairs, please. Supper is ready. He wants to shout, to smash something big like a piano or the steering wheel of an expensive car. He leans, exhausted, into the partly open casement window on the landing.

All at once the triplets and their party visitors are on the stairs, in their excitement, their childish pleasure of exchanging clothes and ornaments. Forcing a smile he nods a greeting, flattening himself against the window frame. There is no sign of the victim or his grotesque Teddy Bear and no sign of Ms Bianca. He runs downstairs. He feels ill.

Recalling a medical condition described in Hazel's *Home Nursing Manual* he takes it from the shelf in the kitchen and goes into his study to read:

On the recognition of manic depressive psychosis, this is an illness most commonly met, these people are low spirited and unable to concentrate, they are talkative and always rushing from one subject to another, quickly becoming destructive . . . and . . .

He remembers his piano and steering-wheel thoughts.

. . . overwhelmed by a sense of their own unworthiness. Restless, anxious and convinced that they will never get better, they are unable to eat or sleep . . .

He reads the next page. Characteristically in alphabetical order the next note explains:

Mattress. Care of;
Mattress is made of non-absorbent durable horse hair covered with strong bed ticking which can be brushed

thoroughly. To protect mattress, cover with long waterproof sheet. To prevent rusting of the mattress from the bed springs, stout covers of sacking, tied to the bedstead with tapes . . .

The Professor feels better at once, as if Hazel has spoken to him; her sensible voice about mattresses would be very soothing. He goes upstairs again. The house does not seem like his house. There is always someone in the bathroom, there was the guest at the beginning of the evening, with some sort of equipment, a tripod and heavy bag. He asked for the bathroom as soon as he stepped into the hall. All evening the bathroom has been occupied. It is strange that visitors want the bathroom. Bathrooms, in his opinion, belonged to the family and the need for them should be taken care of before setting out for a party or whatever . . .

He opens the window on the landing and fondles the bevelled smoothness of the sill. The triplets are no longer on the dance floor. The laughter from the bathroom is unmistakeably theirs. Steam puffs through the little ventilator over the door. There are sounds of other voices, a man's voice, familiar and unwanted (by the Professor).

Out on the lawn the two little orphans are dancing. Cupcake and Sugarbaby have come on from their musical evening and are obviously about to dance with each other's wives. Some of the girls are dancing with each other and two young men, possibly the owners of the Hot Tottie philosophy, seem to be making themselves agreeable.

He runs down to the kitchen, and immediately runs upstairs again; *still the same noises from the bathroom.* He will stay and watch the party from the window and, at the same time, have a good view of the bath-room door.

For the first time this evening he feels more at ease. He thinks of his two friends and their conven-tional good manners which will set a suitable tone for the dance floor. Cupcake and Sugarbaby are forever reliable. Their conversation is always witty, measured and honourable, aspects of their work being applicable to the daily maintenance of the human body. As

Cupcake once said, there are never cadavers with lice. Lice are like rats leaving a sinking ship, lice evacuate the body as death takes over. And, of course, there are no infestations in the bright plastic organs and body parts used nowadays in demonstration lectures.

Today's breakfast, Sugarbaby declares often, is next week's hair and finger nails. An item of astonishing news . . .

'Why are we doing all this?' the Professor asked earlier in the kitchen. This was just when it was discovered that most of the visitors, like the band, were vegetarians. And, as if that was not enough, one of the triplets had changed back into that unsuitable piece of cloth, a bandeau neatly round her thin breasts, and the flesh-coloured bikini panties, shadowed with life-like small creases, suggesting the vulnerable and secret modelling of *the sacred mound, the soft anvil, the workhouse of the world's great trade.*

'Why are we doing all this?' He was aware, then, of an unpleasant petulance in his voice. He repeated his question, ashamed of himself in advance.

'We're celebrating the twenty-firsts,' Hazel said with quiet patience.

'Yes,' Chloë said, 'the twenty-firsts. The girls will remember this evening, this night all their lives.'

'Who could forget it? What lucky person could forget such a nightmare.' The Professor was sorry at once. He wanted to go round the table to kiss them both, to tell them he did not mean what he said. He wanted to hug them both. But Hazel was diving into the oven and Chloë into the freezer. Changing the menu, trying to change the menu, they told him. Food ready to go, they told him. Food ready to go, busy, very busy.

'It's the NEW AGE, Daddy,' the triplet, Amaryllis, she of the deeper, slightly hoarse voice, known especially for her lucid interpretation, years ago, of the vertical slice, explains.

In spite of his relief that the party is a party at last, the Professor feels that it should have been said earlier, all this about drinking only bottled spring water and herb tea. He thinks it very strange that prawns, salami, ham and chicken legs in foil were entirely unacceptable. He remembers clearly, that on their ninth birthday, the triplets had insisted on 'going savoury' and, demanding the sophistication of roast chicken legs wrapped in foil, had ignored the jellies, the individual custard trifles and the little butterfly cakes, all decorated with tiny silver balls making the names, in the pink icing, of all the little girls who were invited to the party . . .

Chloë, hastily spooning cereal and ice-cream into little paper pudding dishes, announces a fresh brewing of camomile tea.

'Oh, goody gum drops!' Hazel relaxes in the ancient and durable idiom, the well-bred accents of their boarding school. She telephones the all-night supermarket and orders more of the little blue and white bottles of iced spring water to be delivered by taxi.

Reflecting on the Victim (in his prolonged absence), the Professor feels sure that he, the Victim, wants to be regarded as an educated man. He even refers to the

Professor, in light-hearted uncalled for conversation, as Odysseus, actually addressing him as Odysseus with frequent mentioning of Penelope forever industrious at her tapestries. Hazel and Chloë take all this with good humour. The Victim, the Incubus, tries to engage the Professor in a classical discussion. Often he stays in his wheelchair by the door of the study and speaks about people being held together by shared family (out-of-date) values and a spurious shared morality. The Professor, feeling that his family is sharing enough, more than enough, maintains (while wondering whether he should take part in the unwanted conversation at all) that people are only held together when they are capable of understanding world-wide moral issues other than simply their own. He takes a cruel, professorial delight in adding that, on the whole, people do not have this capability. Differences are often insoluble, he has said this more than once, irritated by the everlasting presence of this man, the triplets' so-called foundling. Fundamental differences can be understood and, if they are comprehensible, they can ultimately be resolved. He knows that as a professor in a teaching position he should not, in a loud voice, be dogmatic and, in an authoritative manner, end the conversation with the younger man in this way. This whole business of having the rescued Victim as a member of the household has, or should have, come to an end. The Professor pauses in the hall alone with these repetitive non-profitable thoughts.

'Is your mudder and anty a wimmen or a men?' the younger orphan asks the Professor when the two boys come upon him in the gloom of the unlit hall. They are fresh-cheeked after their dancing.

'She is a woman, of course . . .' the Professor is not sure how to reply. 'My mother is a . . .'

'He means Hazill and Chlow,' the elder brother explains.

'Oh, women of course, both of them,' the Professor says quickly, recognising the often apparently asexual appearance and presence of both Hazel and Chloë. 'Both *absolutely* women,' he says with his most reassuring smile.

He knows he will never forget Hazel's calm acceptance on their wedding night. And then, at the appropriate time later, unseen but *imagined*, she allowed herself to be put up in the stirrups and, with the same acceptance, *and* with her valiant good manners, was safely and bravely delivered of the triplets.

There were things, he thinks, not readily dismissed from an attitude of reverence and gratitude towards the woman who was your wife.

'Hazel and Chloë are both women,' he says to the two little boys. 'They are very good women, they are both good and very kind. Kindness is perhaps the most important thing of all.'

If he is honest, the Professor tells himself, he does have these two very good women. They are kind. And, at the same time, he knows he wants, or rather needs, endlessly something else. If he had a pencil on him he would write privately, in pencil, on a scrap of paper, he would write that he wants freedom in love, and more, he wants to be able to love and to be in the presence of someone who loves and wants him. He feels not guilty exactly, but troubled – this is a better word. Because he feels imprisoned, by being husband

and very much father, he feels troubled. He has always been under the impression that, with advancing age, sexual desire waned. Disappeared. But it seems that the opposite is true. Sexual desire, combined with love, is present in complete defiance of age. This note would have to be hidden or thrown away.

$\mathcal{T}$hough they share a small car Ms Bianca has the car more often than Dr Florence. Dr Florence walks or takes the bus, saying that she enjoys both the bus ride and the walk. This, of course, gives the Professor and Dr Florence the chance for special little meetings and journeys either on foot or in the bus. The Professor, not a very competent driver, enjoying a sense of freedom from responsibility, is pleased for Hazel and Chloë to have the unwieldy family car most of the time.

Ms Bianca came to the party by car, Dr Florence will be coming on the late bus, her own wish.

Hazel, noticing that the Professor has exhausted himself with responsibility over the party, tells him to go and meet the late bus. The fresh air, she says, will make him feel better. The main birthday cake will be cut on his return with Dr Florence. The cake will wait . . .

On his way out the Professor sees that Cupcake and Sugarbaby are dancing together with tender good manners. He watches them for a little and they, after the conventional little bow and curtsey (Sugar), move together to the rattan circle where they invite two of the rather plain, shy girls to the next dance.

Hazel suggested, as he was leaving, that the triplets should have their musical requests ready for the band and that Amaryllis should invite the band in for a sit-down vegetarian supper before embarking on the chosen music.

Almost at once the Professor, in the restfulness of walking in the darkness between the street lamps and, while he is, in his mind, thanking Hazel for her everlasting thoughtfulness, he remembers unwillingly the ugly and sinister conversation he heard earlier. He feels he must go back at once and find the uninvited guests and get rid of them. A responsibility which he is unable to disregard. This is particularly difficult when he had been hoping that the bus would come by without Dr Florence and he would have reason to walk on and take her by surprise at her house.

The hot-tottie-cunt territory talk is not easy to put out of the mind; for one thing it has its own poetic rhythm and persistence. And, as well, there is the thought of the man in the raincoat who came early in the evening. He was positively staggering under the weight of a heavy bag and a bundle of awkward tripod sticks which he almost dropped, as they knocked and scratched everything he passed on his way to the *bathroom — requested* as soon as he stepped into the house. He was not rude exactly but had about him an ill-mannered familiarity. That man must still be in the bathroom. The Professor is amazed at his own incompetence. Who else would let a perfect stranger occupy on arrival, and onwards, the bathroom? He thinks nervously of the hand-painted cherubs on the porcelain bath and on the panels of the walls. And then there are the pretty antique brass taps and fittings especially installed . . . He is not in love with the bathroom but he feels he has, in some caddish way, humiliated and cheapened its existence. When at the time, he had questioned the weight and the sheer awkwardness of the equipment (that being the only way he could think of describing it), the man in the raincoat simply explained that he was used to it, it being a great part of his life.

## RAINCOAT MAN SPENDS DAY IN BATHROOM
*'I gave him access,' bewildered Professor admits ...*

All these thoughts and reminders of his duty towards the family, the friends and the party in general are spoiling the silence and the sweet grassy fragrance of the night.

## RAINCOAT MAN SPENDS DAY WITH TRIPOD
## IN BATHROOM
## PROFESSORIAL WIFE SPEAKS OUT WITH
## SISTER
*My husband is a gentleman*
*My brother-in-law is a gentleman*

Instead of turning back he walks on. Hazel and Chloë will deal with uninvited guests, he convinces himself, telling himself that Hazel and Chloë will simply appear as a *presence* and the *unwanted* will leave at once. He knows that the two women together have tremendously successful ways of dealing with any kind of problem.

He thinks once more of the moment of arrival on the familiar and, if he is honest, beloved doorstep.

It would be especially sweet to rouse Dr Florence if, after marking a pile of essays, she has drifted off into a well-deserved and innocent sleep. It is this innocence and her unpossessed and inexperienced body and mind which he longs to awaken. He longs to hold her and to slowly undress her, carefully with great tenderness. Above all, he wants to surprise her and please her with his own experience. He, in the night like this, could imagine himself to be Don Giovanni setting out to serenade and seduce Elvira's maid, except that the Don, having been recently thwarted sexually, has, because of this, the more power. Love, he thinks, the passions, only come *after* we have read the great poetry, that is, when the mind is more mature and then the experience of the poetry is the more wonderful and overwhelming. There is, too, the special quality about being the lover. It seems, to him, that instead of being weaker and less able with the advancing years, the passion and the awe accompanying love and desire seem to be in greater evidence, with greater intensity than earlier. Occupied with pleasing thoughts, the Professor walks fast and with a springy step.

All at once the memories of the ugly words and the ugly intentions nag at him and spoil the serenity of the suburban night. He supposes he should go back at once.

As a counter-irritant he begins, from habit, to lift his tiredness and dutiful thoughts by thinking of Hazel and of his marriage. They have a large comfortable house, large gardens with hedges, lawns, trees, flowers and fruits. They can have large parties. They can sit in the garden and Hazel and Chloë can endlessly plant and sow and cut and weed . . .

. . . It is not difficult for him to look at all these things and to find all the possessions and the accessories of marriage and housekeeping to be simply wearisome and superficial and a barrier to the life he would prefer. He begins to count up the clothes, the hats, the collar studs, the school clothes, the visits to the hairdresser and to the dentist. He thinks of the stupid comparisons people make. And he thinks about jealousy and loneliness, yes, loneliness in marriage and devotion which strangles. Poverty, he thinks of money and that there might not be enough. He allows himself an intake of breath and something like a sob, alongside a cultivated artificial smile of false bitterness, and immediately dislikes himself intensely for this act of emptiness which drains away the passion and awe he was nursing for Dr Florence. For what purpose is this empty self-pity filling his mind? He even imagines that, after the party, no pretty little-girl daughter will come to him and, putting her hand in his, will thank him for her birthday party . . . He tells himself he is never thanked for anything.

He allows himself the moment when Dr Florence, in her nightdress, opens the front door, surprised to see

him but quietly pleased, very pleased that he has
come. The thought is almost too exquisite. The perfect
time, of course, to telephone for a taxi, Flaubert's Cab
Drive, a wild ride back to the party celebrations, *the
long way round* . . .


The shy girls, dressed as if from Hazel's cutting-out
scissors, in contrast to the bits of coloured material
slapped at random on to his daughters' naked bodies,
the half circle of rattan furniture, the orphans dancing
and the voices in crude conversation on the path below
the landing window, all this comes back to him in a
rush. His daughters, 'fashion babes' they call themselves,
'dressed in undress'. They, his callow daughters, actually know and understand things which he does not
know. He knows that however much they know they
are vulnerable.

In his mind he sees Hazel and Chloë standing in
the sun glow of evening, like two mature pears, side
by side, at the far end of the kitchen table while, at
the same time, he recalls Dr Florence and her shy, low

voice telling him that she likes him more than she should, that, in fact, she loves him.

'I am not able to give you all the love you ought to have,' he remembers his reply, wise and lovingly gentle.

And then there were tears, more than once there have been tears, he remembers the tears. He remembers as well another of Mozart's operas, *Honour must be preserved and you have to live with your mistakes* . . . some honest wisdom about responsibility in an aria from *Così fan tutte*. He felt, at the time, wise and loving, and knows that he wants Dr Florence more than anything for himself. Somewhere, he read, that Mozart is loved by the uneducated and by the cultured, by the naïve and by the sophisticated. But all love him for different, and yet the same, reasons; sensual love satisfied . . .

*You have to live with your mistakes*, a form of advice, he realises, which cannot be ignored, especially the romantic music cannot be ignored.

The Professor turns and hurries back the way he has come. Some terrible thing might be happening or might have already happened in his absence. He should not have deserted his house while so much was going on there.

As he reaches his house he passes two aprons, usually devoted to the bodies of Hazel and Chloë but abandoned, now hanging carelessly as if thrown off and into the hedge by the side gate. Once inside the garden, he walks round the house. The band, well fed, is in full force. The dance floor, ruining that part of the lawn, is crowded. Hazel and Chloë, taking up considerable space, are dancing with distinguished guests, the university Master of Music and the emeritus Professor of Maths. Hazel was good at Math. She always left the 's' off, declaring that was the way of the Americans. She maintained that Math is the only honest pursuit of learning, there being no hypocrisy, no pretence, within the boundaries of the particular study. The honest and rational rules appealed to Hazel, the Professor was perfectly able to understand this, thus making it easy for her to continue to hold a rather charming opinion of her favourite subject.

Running upstairs, two at a time, the Professor hears shrieks of laughter from the bathroom, the sounds of male and female laughter mixing with the sound of running water and splashing. One of the voices heard earlier from the garden seems to be very like the voice of the Victim. He thinks he hears another known voice, possibly one of the voices heard earlier, the unwanted fragments of stupid, unrealistic conversation.

He takes up his previous position, on the bend of the staircase by the landing window. He is able to see the band, clearly lit up, and the dancing couples. Should anyone speak while walking on the path he will hear what is said. Further sounds from the bathroom (which is locked) he will hear easily. And if someone emerges from the bathroom, he will, with a swift movement up two treads of the stairs, see who it is – at once.

'That woman!' Two girls are strolling on the path below.

'That woman, Ms Bianca, she's totally hot for the photographer. She needs, if you ask me, a good hammering.'

'Yeah, makes out she's younger than she is.'

'Well, the photographer's no chicken. He's well known. Does a lot of TV stuff. She's onto a good deal!'

Suddenly the bathroom door is unlocked from inside and is wide open. In a cloud of heavily scented steam and immoderate laughter, Ms Bianca, wearing only a bath towel, sprints along the polished floorboards, thoughtlessly leaving wet footprints. She is followed by a man dressed only in wet clinging shorts. He is manipulating an expensive camera. Another man, in a soaked raincoat, is poised with a movie camera, on a tripod, in the space of the open door.

From the door the Professor can see his three daughters, apparently naked, in an overflowing foam bath.

'It's a bubble bath, Daddy.' Amaryllis, surfacing, calls out to the Professor, who, at a loss for words, glances quickly at the scene. He sees the water in pools on the tiles and on the polished boards and all along the landing. 'It's a commercial, Daddy Darling.' Amaryllis is getting out of the bath, her sisters following.

'Oh Daddy, Darling,' the Middle Triplet explains, 'it was a break through for us. We couldn't pass it up. A series of commercials, *Beach and Bathroom*, a series of products, sunscreen, shampoo, conditioner and body oils from "Aphrodite" . . .'

The Professor gazes in amazement at the glistening foam-flecked nakedness.

'*A chilly consciousness of conflicting egoism.* Forgive me, I quote for lack of adequate words.' The stranger, the young man in wet shorts, holding up his camera for a quick picture, continues quickly, 'Sir, we are trespassing. I apologise. We had to work to a deadline and have made excellent footage. May I congratulate you on the beauty of your daughters *and* on this splendid bathroom. You will receive copies of the magazines. And we shall not leave until we have restored your bathroom to its accustomed appearance. A thousand thanks for allowing this intrusion.'

'Thank you,' the Professor remembers his good manners while going back in his mind to the little bunch of newly born babies, rather ugly, with ineffectual tiny wrinkled limbs and unbelievably penetrating voices which, at the time (like the present time), seemed to be saying 'me first, me first' in those unintelligible first inexplicable cryings.

'Does Mother know? About this?' The Professor is amazed at his own question, the present vision disturbingly recreating that earlier never forgotten one.

'She said not to worry you with our work, and guess what!' Amaryllis is pulling a towel from the heated towel rack. 'We had an important appointment early this morning . . . Look, there! Just behind you.'

The Professor, turning, sees a third young man. He recognises the Victim and is surprised to see him standing tall and blond, without his clothes, splints and bandages, and moving with unexpected grace and naked arrogance; his fair skin flushed suddenly, as if with a disturbing surge of feeling and passion, as in certain dramatic passages of music in which the music reaches deified heights, an apotheosis, in fact.

The Professor, noticing this, is all at once filled with a feeling of tenderness for the young man who is obviously aware of the Professor's scrutiny. There is a moment of a recognition of deep feeling between the older man and the younger. The Professor understands at once that he himself is being examined, examined and exposed by the younger man's almost painful rush of heat, a blush in his fair skin, round his neck and ears and gradually spreading down his body.

It is as if the Professor is simply looking for a considerable length of time into a photograph or a painting, without emphasis on any particular aspect of the delicate and susceptible subject offered (other than an emotionally precious moment), in which he is seeing only a vague pink glow of unreachable, for the present, youth.

In spite of the astonishment of the emotional dramatic change of regard towards the young man, the ex-Victim, and the ability to feel and understand this and to be understood, across the floor, from across the other side of the room, a bathroom complete with water splashes and nakedness, the Professor tells himself that he is able to accommodate the spread of material (for want of better description). For, after all, twenty-one years with the triplets did not pass without incidents, something fresh and previously unthought of, which had to be understood or accepted or disposed of. Perhaps more importantly, for the present, nothing was said to suggest anything which took place in the silent recognition.

Acceptance, the Professor tells himself as he goes down to the kitchen, acceptance is something he has learned while collecting and reading essays and other writing by contemporary students whose work reflects so clearly their surroundings, their use of language, ideas created from their reading and observations, even from the lectures they attend – to which they have added their interpretations and natural reactions. To read and mark an essay is, among others things, both a privilege and the posing and the solving of a riddle. More importantly about this evening, and remembering the bitterness he experienced towards the Victim (the Incubus) earlier, the Professor is deeply touched, as if forever, by their recent unspoken, completely silent acknowledgement, the one fully dressed and the other without clothes.

For a moment he pauses to peer into the garden, the party continues as if blossoming with the music and the dancing and the little groups talking and laughing. This evening he feels he has recaptured the triplets by acknowledging their working clothes – foam – in their work place – the elegant bathroom renovated in Victorian style with Queen Victoria's favourite design, the Greek Key, fully in evidence, together with the hand-painted cherubs.

He understands that the bathroom pictures, or photographs, will have been made with the same concentration, the same delicate feeling for art, as in the work of a translator who becomes nearer to his subject than the ordinary reader, and even more so than the author of the work being translated. These pictures, he understands, will offer a closer understanding of the exquisite features and limbs and the deliciously captured movements of the muscles and the bodies *and* the products they are meant to be demonstrating. These will be made as desirable as possible, as in the translation of poetry and prose from the best words in one language to the best words in another language.

The translator who catches the epic tone and preserves the spirit of the original poem in his search for the best word, the satisfying phrase, naturally is nearer to the emotional experience being expressed, by the writer, in the particular work in the first place. The translator, and in the same way, the musician, the performer of some music, can be regarded as being closer to the meaning and the mood than even the writer or the composer. The writer and the composer may even be perplexed by their own works. The same, the Professor thinks, may be true about some aspects of the bathroom scene, the remnants of the scene, it being finished when the door was opened.

*I*t's no use at all you swinging for 'em or going to gaol for any one or all of them, that's what I've always said. For better or for worse, that's my opinion. Down the hatch!' The taxi driver, who earlier delivered the hastily required little bottles of iced spring water, is still sitting at the washed kitchen table with one of Hazel's apple pies, divided into generous portions in front of him.

'I'll tell you,' he repeats, 'it's no use you courtin' the ropes for one of *them*.' The taxi driver, who looks as if he has come to stay the night, makes as if he has a noose tightening round his neck. He takes up the bread knife as if he is about to slash his own throat.

'Ah!' the Professor utters one of his intelligent responses. He has a little store of them, in different lengths and tones, in readiness, always.

Amaryllis and the Victim are both in the kitchen. Amaryllis is mixing a drink, with a dash of the professorial whisky for the young man. There is an air of happiness surrounding the two young people. Amaryllis, putting her small hand into her father's hand, thanks him for the lovely party. She explains that Ms Bianca had taken them earlier in the day, in her car, to the final appointment with the surgeon; and *the Victim together with his Bear* had been pronounced fit and well and able to do anything they wanted to do. Ivor, the Victim, is able to dispense with bandages, splints and wheelchairs.

'So much happened all at once.' Amaryllis, breathless, her little round face pretty and her eyes shining, says, 'We didn't know until the last minute that we had scored the commission for all that advertising, so we couldn't tell you, Daddy, what we were doing. And then Mother said not to worry you. And then Ivor and I got engaged in the bathroom while the filming was going on.'

'Ah!' the Professor, nodding, looks wise.

'Ivor, the Victim,' Amaryllis says. 'Ivor loves

dancing. He's allowed to do anything he feels like. We're just on our way out to the dancing now. I promised Cupcake the tango.'

'Good, Good!' the Professor uses his humorous and quietly encouraging voice. Glancing up, he smiles and is rewarded with a small shy smile in return from the Victim. He has to understand, he tells himself, that the Victim was just a boy anyway and his apparently selfish bad behaviour was probably a complication of fear and shock. Briefly he wonders why he did not understand this earlier.

'I tell you this,' the taxi driver persists, 'it's no use you swinging on the whatsaname, name's gone, it'll come back, no use you swinging ... Well, yes tah, I don't mind if I do.' He pushes his empty glass forward towards the Professor. 'Just a nip, I am on the fuckin' road whether I like it or not. Thank you very much tah!'

The Professor, picking at a few shrivelled prawns, is not clear what the taxi driver means, apart from accepting another drink. He asks for the statement to be repeated, knowing that conducting a seminar for one is about the most laborious duty included within the boundaries of university teaching, often the most tedious and unrewarding . . .

'I'm telling you, sir, it's no use us swinging for 'em . . . *the offspring*. Know what I mean?' The taxi driver once more places the metaphorical noose round his neck and holds the bread knife across his throat.

'Ah!' the Professor has the possibility of several sounds of understanding within the single syllable. In the customary silence, before replying, he thinks, as he sometimes does, of his mother, an Oxford Don (clever and eccentric) of years ago. He remembers that she spoke to her maid, her chauffeur and her gardener as if they were first-year students about to embark on a dramatic reading of *The Aeneid*:

> *There was an ancient city, a colony of Tyre*
> *which stood on the African coast fronting across the sea*

She never started at the beginning but always a little way into the beloved poetry of the epic, in order, she would explain, to offer a familiar image for the presentation of much that would seem unfamiliar. In her well-bred way she would demonstrate how the ardent love between Dido and Aeneas would have to give way to destiny . . .

The Professor, sitting beside the taxi driver in the front seat, has the enlightening thought that where there are two people together, but having nothing in common between them, except sitting together, next to each other and not concerned *the one with the other*, then this is privacy of a particular kind. It is true privacy as neither can discuss the other with anyone since both have no word, each on the other. In this extra and sudden privacy *and* unexpected freedom, the Professor does not have to question the taxi driver, neither does he have to furnish answers should the taxi driver question him.

The taxi driver, intent on pursuing his earlier thought, is in the middle of a speech of general disapproval, saying that every individual should have his own shotgun and should use it, practically, on anyone within range. He interrupts his list of those to be dealt with first, to alter his language for some immediate compliments to be delivered, accompanied by fierce horn blowing, to another taxi which has foolishly attached its bulk as if to travel side by side in what is meant to be single-lane traffic.

But all this is of no concern to the Professor who is comfortable in his curtained privacy (a metaphor which fits very well, he thinks), his thoughts are then taken up by a very sweet moon, previously not noticed.

With a further blasting of horns and voices, the two taxis separate and follow their own ways. The Professor's man, without the need for fresh breath, is back to all the wrongs in present-day society and the salvation in the possession of a gun.

Though this is not the curtained privacy to be found in literature (Flaubert's famous cab), the Professor feels confident and serene for the first time during the evening. It was Hazel's idea that he should fetch Dr Florence, especially since Ms Bianca has gone on to another party, and even more especially, as there is a taxi and a driver at the kitchen door. Destiny? Perhaps, Hazel thought so. He could bring Dr Florence back and she could sleep over in the sitting room. The Professor, feeling grateful to Hazel, tells her not to wait up for him. 'And the same for Chloë,' he adds.

'Chloë's still dancing. You *know* Chloë!' Hazel replies.

Delicious little half-spoken confidences of feeling and little bursts of deeply felt tenderness, the Professor is relaxed in anticipation which is, he thinks, perhaps the only real happiness there is. The approach to happiness . . .

The drive seems very short. The curtained privacy is very restful. Hazel, it seems to the Professor, had relief in her eyes when she was waving the taxi driver out between the gate posts. The Professor, briefly, is sorry that his own agitation during the party will have been a burden on Hazel and on Chloë. He comforts the thought with the real fact that Hazel and Chloë always shared misfortune and so only suffered, half each, of any difficulty.

When he arrives and when he has paid the driver, he will go up the path, in the pure moonlight, to the front door. And when Dr Florence opens the door, he will take her in his arms with tenderness. They will pause and wait for the taxi to turn and drive off.

Dr Florence will probably try to apologise and explain about her absence from the party. She might even try to explain about her 'break up', devastating even if only temporary, with Ms Bianca. Quickly he will close the front door and dismiss Ms Bianca's latest 'fling' as being 'ill-bred, ungentlemanly and only a photographer, forget him!'

He will kiss her hands, her arms, her neck and her lips. With his arm round her, and feeling the soft material of her gown in between his fingers, he will guide her up the rather small staircase.

He will be prepared for her tears, her shyness and even her fear. He will whisper and breathe her gown away. She will try to cover herself but he will explain that it is right for them to be naked. He will slowly approach as the lover, gradually, with all his power held in restraint until he feels the moment of penetration and her acceptance accompanied by the little sigh which requires no explanation. With increasing power he will . . .

'That'll be fifteen dollars, thank you.' The driver swings his taxi up on to the grass outside the university apartments. The Professor fumbles for change and pays the driver. He steps through the hedge and walks along the concrete slabs of path and knocks on the door of Dr Florence's apartment. He feels nervous; his fumbling for the taxi money worries him just when he needs to be, like the conductor of an orchestra, in command, but gently. The moonlight casts shadows and the rosemary hedge he brushed against has a clean healthy fragrance. He is anxious for the door to be opened. He hopes a light will show, soon, in one of the few windows.

In his nervousness the Professor lets thoughts come without being able to control them. This visit, this evening, he thinks, possibly it should never take place. Once you feel desire for someone, the real wish for someone, and you experience real love, you want it again and then there is another time and another. It is not a simple meeting which then ends all meetings. He, in his wisdom, thinks he should not stay but should go at once and walk home in the moonlight. The door opens as he is about to leave. Dr Florence, caught in the soft light of the street lamp and the light in her hall, gives a little cry of pleasure at seeing him, and he, at once, steps into the hall taking her in his arms.

Gently with one arm round her, the Professor reaches back to close the front door with his other hand. Feeling the soft material of her gown with sensitive fingers he guides her up the narrow stairs. Everything, except the silky softness of the gown yielding to his hands, slips from his thoughts.

He whispers and breathes her gown away and, when she tries to cover herself, he laughs and assures her that, for this, they must be naked.

It is at this moment of secretly drawn breath that the flute player, after hovering in perfect restraint before giving full sound to the wordless adoration, receives the longed for single glance of recognition and intention from the conductor.

He wants to tell her that his body is worshipping her body. He wants to speak to her of his reverence, his admiration, his deep fondness, his love for her and his complete tender understanding of her needs *and* his own deeply felt gratitude from which it will be impossible to turn away.

At the same time he feels he should speak about an all too easily imagined but realistic restlessness and unhappiness, a *painful reality when they have to be apart*. He, with a small groan, nestles his head between her breasts, feeling at the same time the return of desire. He holds in his thoughts the imagined but real picture of the tender glance of questioning and the readily given approval passing between the flute player and the conductor.

This glance occurring, as it does, when the flute player opens his eyes after a particularly difficult and responsible passage in the music, in which he is maintaining exquisite harmony with the pianist, is a gaze from beneath the half-closed swollen eyelids and is, once again, the evidence for the conductor to match with tender experience and need.

$\mathcal{B}$eing in turn refreshed, light-hearted and youthful, the Professor and Dr Florence, in the morning, set off to walk to the Professor's house. The Professor, hugging Dr Florence in the middle of the quiet road, boasts that he, like Teiresias, the blind prophet, is able to inhabit and understand exactly a woman's desire, her need and experience in lovemaking.

Dr Florence, weeping suddenly, declares that she is not practised in comparison with his perfect and sweet performance. Also, she does not want to leave him or him to leave her.

The Professor, appalled at his own conceit, tells her that she is perfect, and that they will be together all day.

In the ensuing silence the Professor wonders if Ms Bianca will be returning at once, or later or not at all. He feels he will never forget the sight of her, in a bath towel, being chased by that undressed, scruffy individual with his camera. Having to see the ugly, the commonplace, the ridiculous and the squalid alongside his daughters can be compared with having to know and understand that the burned and rendered offal from slaughtered, emaciated, drought-ridden cattle is used in the form of gelatine in the making of the smooth white purity of vanilla ice-cream. In any case why was Ms Bianca trying to push herself in on the making of the 'commercials', his daughters' word, not his own.

But why think of Ms Bianca when all he wants, just now, is to think of and talk to Dr Florence and to walk with her held close to him. He would like, he tells her, to lie down with her, hidden in the long grass of a deserted house.

All is quiet in the garden of the Professor's house. Small heaps of party rubbish are neatly by the back gate. Some balloons lie on the grass and the rattan circle of shabby garden chairs are waiting to be put away. The crushed grass of the lawns sweetens the morning.

Peering into the little boys' tent the Professor understands that this is one of the many meeting places of the different worlds they all inhabit. Some of the times of meeting are easily absorbed but for others, *the other*, it is not so simple. There is really no choice, which world? No choice! He feels himself crying some- where inside. Dr Florence quietly puts her hand on his hand. He takes her in his arms.

'I have not behaved well,' he says in a low voice. 'I'm sorry. I have been incredibly selfish.'

'Oh, please don't say or think that,' Dr Florence says, 'we must not have regrets!' They kneel down by the open end of the tent and pull the thick blanket down over the red-and-blue ribbed socks of the sleep- ing occupants.

'They must have been sick during the night.' The Professor indicates two plastic buckets next to the little boys. He wants to tell Dr Florence that, stupidly, he piled up their plates with pickles and cold meat. 'They are so obedient, they eat all they are given!' he says softly. 'I have been such a fool!' He wants to tell her that in so many ways he has been stupid and selfish. He wants to talk about love and how Capellanus, in the twelfth century, described love as *a certain inborn suffering derived from the sight of an excessive meditation upon the beauty of the opposite sex, which causes each one to wish above all things the embraces of the other and by common desire to carry out all of love's precepts in the other's embrace . . .*

Hazel comes from the house. She explains to the kneeling lovers that the little boys were very sick but they rushed indoors to fetch a bucket each. Hazel laughs. 'We're very impressed, Chloë and I,' she says. She goes on to say that they will never forget how the triplets vomited everywhere when they were little girls. It was a question of bathing them in the night and washing their hair and changing their bed clothes. The Prof. would remember because he was very noble and was up out of bed to do his share, every time.

'But you must come indoors,' Hazel says gently to Dr Florence, 'you must have a rest. You're tired.'

The Professor does remember the triplets when

they were little girls. He had no idea then of all the difficulties which accompany the rearing of children. They, the difficulties of growing up, of living, are endless.

The Professor, left to himself by the little boys' tent, looks once more at their small feet in the crudely coloured ribbed socks. He feels ineffectual and sad and unable to go on to witness the pain of the shy inexperienced boy blundering on into being a man – without the necessary explanations and examples, for how can anyone offer either explanations or examples unless the particular need is clearly seen, or asked for.

He walks about the trampled lawn for half an hour for he must have the adequate words for explanation for Hazel. And, at the same time, is not sure if any explanation will be needed. Hazel must be his chief concern now.

He feels tender and exposed. Music, he thinks, would run fast over words clearly like spring water over pebbles, so that when it comes to talking about intimate details of lovemaking it is not needed to splash words in praise of the soft anvil, the neat virginal mons, to the wrong woman, for these words might be owing to the rightful (by law) woman but, in fact, really belong to the woman whose body is being worshipped. Music is applicable to words in order to create harmony (if only he could sing, something from Mozart, expressing desire). A soothing approach is needed to prepare the state of mind which, being imaginative, will see facts and images not related to the music but to life itself.

He supposes he can trust himself and Hazel with complete full understanding, each one of the other.

Hazel returns quite soon. The Professor sees at once that her eyelids are reddened and swollen. It is not the first time that he has seen tears trembling, without falling, from her eyelashes. Even though Hazel would always claim responsibility for her tears, the Professor knows that he, during the years, has mostly been the cause of them.

He could say that Hazel sent him to Dr Florence because she could feel the need in both of them for each other. He would never dream of blaming her for giving him the chance to love Dr Florence, to 'make love' to Dr Florence.

And she, Hazel, would never accuse him of being the lovesick clown who needed to be despatched to his beloved, unreachable without help from an accommodating spouse.

Neither of them would sink to the shameful, both believing that marriage is based on passion and awe in whatever form and direction these take. Marriage, both believe that a marriage cannot be successful if supported only by forgiveness.

They stand together at the kitchen end of the lawns. Hazel says the grass, even the grass ruined under the dance floor, will pick up quite quickly. The Professor likes the idea of Hazel making the grass a symbol, especially in the suggestion of a quick recovery.

Hazel says then that she is sure that there isn't anything between them which cannot be managed.

She says to him to come in for breakfast. Chloë is frying potato cakes. And she leaves him to brood for a bit on her skilful use of the double negative . . .

The Professor's choice for a quotation. He requests:

*There is nothing in all Damascus . . . half so well seeing as our cellars; and forthwith he invited me to go, see, and admire the long range of liquid treasure that he and his brethren had laid up for themselves on earth. And these, I soon found, were not as the treasures of the miser that lie in unprofitable disuse; for day by day, and hour by hour, the golden juice ascended from the dark recesses of the cellar to the uppermost brains of the friars . . . in the midst of that solemn land, their Christian laughter rang loud and merrily — their eyes kept flashing with joyful fire, and their heavy woollen petticoats could no more weigh down the springiness of their paces than the filmy gauze of a* danseuse *can clog her bounding step.*

(*Eothen*, by A. W. Kinglake, 1844.)

*H*azel's choice, supported by Chloë, for a quotation
to follow the Professor's choice.

### THE HERB OF SELF-HEAL

*This herb it is called prunel, or carpenter's herb, hook-heal*
*and fickle wort.*

*The common self-heal is a small low creeping herb with many*
*small round, and at the same time, pointy leaves, rather like*
*the leaves of the wild mints, they are a dark green in colour,*
*without any dents on the edges, from among which rise divers*
*small leaves and small stalks with leaves creeping upon the*
*ground.*

*PLACE: It is found in woods and fields everywhere in this*
*kingdom.*

*TIME: It flowereth in May, sometimes in April.*

*This is an herb of Venus. It is a special herb for inward and outward wounds . . . to cleanse the foulness of sores and cause them to be speedily healed, cleaneth and healeth all ulcers of the mouth and throat from what cause so ever.*

*It is taken inwardly in syrups for inward wounds and outwardly in unguents and plaisters . . .*

(*The English Physician and Complete Herbal*, Vol. I, by Nicholas Culpeper, 1700s.)

ACKNOWLEDGEMENTS

An earlier version of pages 38 to 79 was published as 'An Intellectual Father' in the *New Yorker*, 29 July 1996.

The author wishes to acknowledge the use of the following.

'Heraclitus', a poem by William J. Cory, in *Golden Treasury of Songs and Lyrics* (Book 5) selected and edited by Laurence Binyon, Macmillan, London, 1928 (p. 20); letter written by Gilbert Burnet to the Earl of Halifax, as quoted in *The Debt to Pleasure* by John Adlard, Carcanet Publishing, Cheadle, 1974 (p. 46); 'Song', a poem by John Wilmot, in *The Debt to Pleasure*, (pp 51, 52, 89); 'The Salutation', a poem by Thomas Traherne, in *Seventeenth Century Prose and Poetry*, selected and edited by Robert P. Tristram and Alexander M. Wintherspoon, Harcourt Brace and Company, New York, 1929 (p. 53); John Wilmot, as quoted in *The Debt to Pleasure* (p. 54); 'The Rules of Courtly Love' by Andreas Capellanus, as quoted in *The Portable Medieval Reader*, edited by James Bruce Ross and Mary Martin McLaughlin, Viking Press, New York, 1949 (P. 103); letter written by John Wilmot, Earl of Rochester, to his wife, as quoted in *The Debt to Pleasure* (p. 106); *The Taming of the Shrew* by William Shakespeare, Swan Shakespeare edition, J. M. Dent, London, 1930 (p. 157, 175, 176); *Confessions* (Book X) by St Augustine, edition edited by Betty Radice and Robert Baldick, Penguin Books Ltd, London, 1961 (p. 164, 165); *The Aeneid* by Virgil, edited by Patrick Dickinson, Mentor Classics, New English Library Limited, London, 1961 (p. 234); *Eothen*, by A. W. Kinglake, J. M. Dent, London, 1844 (p. 251); *The English Physician and Complete Herbal*, Vol. I, by Nicholas Culpeper, London, 1700s (p. 253).